Fettered Love

~~ Stories of Courage ~~

Vernella Fuller

St. James, Jamaica

books@fruithillpress.com

A catalogue record for this book is available from the National Library of Jamaica.

e-book ISBN: 978-976-95911-1-0

pbk ISBN: 978-976-95911-0-3

DEDICATION

For my dearest daughter Alisha Nadine, my beloved late grandmother Beatrice, my dear parents; my late father Joselcyn and my mother Delceta.
There is no greater legacy than the gift of love.

CONTENTS

Dedication
Acknowledgements

ACKNOWLEDGMENTS

Writing is a labour of love, and writing this collection of stories has been a wonderful love affair. I am grateful for the encouragement I receive from my daughter, Alisha Nadine. She has been my inspiration and will always be a part of the reason why I write.

I would also like to thank Sandra Ferconio for her thorough and insightful editing, her attention to detail and her tenacious work ethic.

I am inspired by the lives, passions, and triumphs of courageous people. This book is about the courage of the human spirit to love, endure, and even prosper against adversity. I am grateful to all the women I have met, have known, or may never know who have had the courage to love, endure, and prosper against adversity.

1 DAYS OF CHAMPAGNE AND ROSES

If you think you are free,
there is no escape possible.
~ Ram Dass ~

Carleen was fifteen and on her way to school when Len first called out to her from the driver's seat of his BMW 5 Series. She was living in Saint Catherine and had passed her Common Entrance, winning a scholarship to one of the prestigious high schools in Kingston. Carleen liked the way she felt when he slowed his car and picked her out from her friends, asking her to behave herself and study hard in school. Even at fifteen years old, she could tell his mouth was saying those words but his eyes were saying something entirely different. For her part, the swing of her slim, shapely hips became more pronounced as she walked away. Feeling his eyes on her back, she fought to control the smile that overwhelmed her.

Len hired Carleen to work in his office during the following summer vacation. This pleased Carleen's mother especially since Carleen was paid the same salary as a full-time, permanent office staff. Her mother called him a good man and told Carleen that if she wanted to attend university she had to please him. Her mother had a unique way of making these types of suggestive statements. Carleen had heard her mother make similar statements to her older sister when her sister was in high school. Carleen had met the good man who her sister had been nice to and later married. Her mother would lower her voice, feign an innocent expression, and then sharply say, "You better get my meaning." Then, as if to make sure, she would add, "Life is hard here in Jamaica, and you are lucky to have the looks to get you through."

Carleen was careful to tell friends who knew of their relationship that nothing had happened between her and Len until after she turned sixteen. By the time she turned sixteen, she was working full-time as his personal assistant in his music-promotion business. She wanted to attend university full-time, but he said he would only pay for her to go part-time. At that time, he offered her a permanent job in his office and told her that the full-time position was only available now. He would not hold the position for five years until she finished all of her university courses.

She called her years from fifteen to eighteen—days of champagne and roses. "He is incredibly generous and kind," she had boasted to her best friend, Peta-Gaye.

When she was with him in those days, she didn't remember or think about the other girls he was rumoured to have had. Eventually, Carleen found out that Len was married, but she had a fantasy that when the time was right he would leave his wife. While she was Len's lover, she knew that a boyfriend was out of the question; he did not say so in so many words—but she knew, she just knew.

In the office and around the other office staff, they never displayed affection towards one another. She understood by his body language that showing signs of affection in public was not acceptable. His only outward show of preference towards her was her use of the adjoining office. She had a private office and did not have to share it with any of the other office-staff members.

For the first few years, she was not threatened by any of the other lovers he was rumoured to have had. He told her she was special to him, and she knew it was true.

He paid her well at work, gave her presents outside of work, and helped her mother. Len's generosity towards Carleen and her mother was especially helpful with unforeseen expenses that they could not have taken care of on their own. Her mother's housekeeping work helped, but it was not enough. If her sister's husband, and now Len, had not helped out the family over the years, they would not have been able to make ends meet.

Len's wife never visited the office, so in Carleen's consciousness Len's wife was an inconsequential shadow. Len mentioned her infrequently, and when he did he only used short, dismissive phrases.

Carleen saw Len's wife once a year at his annual international music show. Len always assigned Carleen duties in his VIP booth at the show. His wife would be there with her girlfriends and senior staff who worked in the beauty business that she owned on the other side of the island. Len was always in the box too surrounded by his entourage.

Carleen found herself staring at Len's wife when she was sure her staring was unnoticed. She had clearly been beautiful in her day, Carleen thought. Her individual features were stunning: flawless, dark-brown skin; wide eyes; a full, shapely mouth; and a button-like nose. She looked young for her age and spoke in a soft quiet voice that made everyone listen when she spoke. Carleen was captivated by her, and it seemed that so was everyone else around her. But Len would only say of her, "De woman come get fat pan me." Carleen had no affection for his wife, but she was offended by Len's disdain for his wife's weight gain.

Carleen finished high school and felt like the mature woman Len said she was turning into, but he showed no sign of making her the number one woman in his life as he had constantly promised over the years.

Carleen heard rumours that when he had a good year with his show he bought extravagant gifts for women. For his favoured women, it was rumoured that he gave them cars or took them with him on some of his frequent trips abroad. It was even mentioned that he had fathered two children outside of his marriage. She did not feel she could ask him (let alone challenge him) about the rumours. When she could bear to entertain such thoughts, she rationalized that she had been inferior from the start and could never hope to be his equal. Given all of the women she knew (educated and uneducated), they all seemed to accept a lower position than their partner's position in relationships—this was what she understood as the woman's rightful position.

~~~~~

At the age of twenty-three and finally finished with her university studies, Carleen secretly decided that she would give the relationship two more years. She had told him she wanted to have a child. He dismissed the idea saying he was not ready to have children with her yet.

"I want you to stay just the way you are now. Having a baby changes a woman's body, and I don't want anything about you to change. I want you to stay as you were when you were sixteen," he had told her.

The two years she had secretly allotted to the relationship quickly passed, and there was no change in their relationship. He was still attentive when they were in private together, and he continued to look after her and her mother. She continually rehearsed in her head how she would tell him the relationship was over: *It has to end, unless*…. But she never found the strength to utter the words. And what would she do without him? The men in her age group knew she was his girl, so men never glanced at her. They knew (even more than she knew) Len had an uncanny sense to spot anything more than a cursory glance in her direction. There had been a few glances by a few daring men over the years. But who could she find? Even if she dared an affair, she knew most men were afraid of Len, and the men who surrounded him competed for his favour by being his eyes and ears. There were no secrets from Len.

On her first trip abroad, Len took her to Miami to celebrate ten years together and her twenty-fifth birthday. As always, she boasted to her friends that he gave her the best time in every way possible.

On the first Monday after they returned, a woman from England appeared in the office looking for Len. He was not in the office when the woman arrived, and she insisted that no one call him. With a smile on her face, she said she would wait for him. For an hour or so she waited in the reception area, reading magazines, newspapers, and a book she had brought with her. Curiosity overwhelmed not only Carleen but also everyone in the office.

When Len finally arrived, he was clearly stunned to see the English woman. He stood for several moments looking at her and shaking his head. She smiled broadly without speaking, and eventually they hugged. While holding her around her waist and leading her to his office, his laughter and exclamations resounded throughout the office.

The woman's name was Rachael, and she was not young like so many of Len's other favoured women. Carleen had heard that Rachael was in her forties and a couple of years older than Len.

It soon became clear that Rachael's age was not the only thing that was different between her and the other women who hung around Len. Rachael was an educated woman, a professor of some sort. Carleen also heard that she owned property abroad and an apartment in the affluent hills of Kingston. Over the next six weeks, she appeared in the office two or three times a week, always without an appointment or warning.

All eyes fastened on her when she glided into the office with her ready smile, thin toned body, flawless ebony complexion, and immaculate dress and manners. Unlike the other women who had to wait in the reception area, she tapped lightly on his office door and entered.

She never stayed long, and she exited his office as nonchalantly as she had entered, smiling as she bade farewell to the staff. Carleen's eyes would follow her on the closed-captioned monitor as she slid into her waiting car. Len never left with her. He would leave shortly after her and not return to the office for the rest of the day.

Over the next few years, it was quickly established that when Rachael was on the island there were no calls to Carleen for her to meet him in their favourite hotel room. There were no weekend getaways to the north coast, and he did not drop by at her mother's house.

After Carleen told her mother about Rachael, her mother also understood what was happening and did not ask about Len when she knew Rachael was in town. She encouraged her daughter to be patient, reminding her that Len always called her after Rachael left. "You know you hold the special place beside his wife," her mother counselled.

Peta-Gaye was adamant that they should find out about the mysterious woman. The girls had heard bits and pieces of rumours. They had heard that Len and Rachael began their affair in Jamaica many years earlier while Rachael was on holiday with her husband. It was rumoured that her husband found out long after they had started their affair. Suspecting an affair, he secretly followed her on one of the holiday trips to Jamaica and found her with Len. Somehow their marriage survived for several more years, but now Carleen had heard that they were divorced.

Even though Len and Rachael's affair had started before Len and Carleen met, Carleen was amazed that she had not heard anything about it until now. Carleen wondered whether they had stopped their affair when Len and her first met and whether Rachael had been with him on some of those frequent trips abroad: she supposedly working at her marriage, and he supposedly travelling on business.

Peta-Gaye said she did not understand what an educated, refined woman like Rachael saw in a womanising ruffian like Len. Carleen, shocked by her friend's comment, hung her head in silence.

When Rachael was on the island, Len was clearly different around the office: He was preoccupied, even wistful. The staff often gossiped about it, and the especially spiteful staff expressed their views loud enough for Carleen to hear. The office staff couldn't put it into words, but they all understood that Rachael was not like the others.

Carleen longed to see him and Rachael together outside of the crowded office. She wanted to work out for herself what Len found so special about the English woman. One year as the annual jazz festival was approaching, Carleen got her chance. She overheard Len telling one of his friends that Rachael had arrived on the island for the festival. Carleen's heart sank. Since Carleen and Len had been together, he had always bought a VIP box for himself and his entourage and had given Carleen two tickets (one for her and one for Peta-Gaye). Then after the jazz festival, he always met Carleen at their special hotel for the weekend.

This time he did not mention tickets to her, and he hardly glanced at her. She was inconsolable. Peta-Gaye persuaded Carleen that they should buy their own tickets and go together. Carleen was reluctant. Although she wanted to see them together, she was afraid he would get angry if he thought she was following him around after he had not invited her.

"You don't know what you want. I thought you wanted to see them together," Peta–Gaye said, "even though I have never understood why. You can't still believe they are just good friends. Anyway, you might not even see them there. There are thousands of people at the show," Peta-Gaye warned her friend, "and if you do, it's only going to upset you."

"How can I be upset?" Carleen said bitterly. "He is married...had his wife when we met, and some say lots of other women too. I have always known the score," Carleen lamented.

Peta-Gaye and Carleen arrived at the hotel in the early afternoon; after eating and napping, they got ready for the first evening of the three-night jazz festival.

Peta-Gaye shook her head. "But he clearly loves this one. And here's me thinking all along that a man like him was not capable of love."

"I know you have always hated him," Carleen responded.

"Of course," her friend said, without apology, "he is a pompous, ignorant man who thinks he is more than he is. Some girls only go for him because he has money and (if truth be told) because he seduces them. Others …" she hesitated, "others because they were too young when it started and got into the mess before they had the sense to know what was happening."

Peta-Gaye only realised that her friend was crying after Carleen did not respond. She tried hard to soften her voice, but there was no softness in her heart. "Haven't I been telling you for years that if you expect more than you've been getting, you are going to upset yourself?"

After being at the show for a few hours, circling the venue several times, feigning interest in the various concessionary stalls, and praying she would bump into him, she decided to take one last stroll. She left an exasperated Peta-Gaye to guard their seats. She had just manoeuvered away from the main stage, away from the thickest part of the crowd, when she saw Len and Rachael approaching hand-in-hand towards her.

In all the years they had been together, he had not once held her hand in public. Holding hands was not one of the things he did—not with her, not with anyone. Carleen could hardly lift her feet as she approached them. She burnt with anxiety and rage. It crossed her mind that to spare her he might pass without acknowledging her presence. Maybe Rachael would not recognize her out of the context of the office.

"Hello, Carleen," he said with ease, as they came face-to-face.

"Hello, Mr. Len."

Dropping Rachael's hand and pulling her into a side embrace, he said, "You know Dr. Rachael."

"Enjoy the show," Dr. Rachael said, with a smile as they sidestepped around her and moved on.

Carleen turned to watch them weave their way through the crowd once again hand-in-hand. It was several minutes before she was able to move.

~~~~~

Rachael returned to her home in England soon after the jazz festival ended. During the next few months, Carleen and Len only saw each other in the office, and they only talked about work—that was the extent of their contact. Then after three months, Len called Carleen and asked her to meet him at their favourite hotel.

In the three months that she waited for him to call, she dreamt about what she would say and how she would say it. How would she say, *No thank you, I don't want to be with you anymore.* Most weekends her mother could not persuade her to leave her room. She ate almost nothing and cried without provocation. Her mother warned her that she would lose her looks; then there would be no hope.

On Monday, full of hope again, she did her best by dressing in a way that had previously led to a surreptitious midday call for her to meet him in their room at the hotel. On Friday, the call finally came. The heavy pain that had crippled her heart eased a little, and she was so grateful for the release. She spoke only to agree to the time.

When she got to the hotel, he was already there—showered, stripped to the waist, and lying under the covers. "Go and take a shower and then come and rub down my back," he said. "My shoulders are tense. I need a massage bad."

She wanted to say, *You have never given me a massage. My whole body is tense and has been tense for months.* But she said nothing and did as he had asked. She was exhausted when he was ready for her to stop.

He ordered her favourite meal from room service: grilled salmon, mashed potatoes, and a green salad. She drank white wine, and he had white rum chased with iced water.

She ached to talk about Rachael, but she knew she dare not.

They did not make love until Saturday night, and after they did he said he needed to sleep alone. By his words, she understood that she had to leave. It was well past midnight when he called one his friends to take her home. He told her not to return on Sunday: He wanted to be alone.

Rachael returned at least twice a year for the next few years: at Easter and in the summer. Once she stayed for a whole year. She was on a sabbatical, Carleen had heard. During that year, Len did not once call Carleen. After the sabbatical, Len left with Rachael when she went back to England, and he spent over three months there.

"He is continuing to make a complete idiot of you," Peta-Gaye insisted. Peta-Gaye was now married with two children. "Why are you doing that to yourself? Why do you hate yourself so much? At least get yourself a lover."

Carleen knew that taking a lover was not possible. Perhaps Len no longer cared if she did, but she did not know how to go about that anymore. "I decided my fate when I gave myself to him at fifteen, and now I have to live with that decision," she told her friend.

Whether Rachael was on the island or on the phone calling from another country, her presence pervaded the office. Carleen always knew when Len was on the phone with Rachael. More than once Len invited Carleen in his office as he finished his call with Rachael. "You know we will be spending our old age together," he would say to Rachael, in a tone he had never used with Carleen. Carleen knew that he was sincere about Rachael. He did not waste words saying things he did not mean.

Len still looked after Carleen, giving her occasional gifts and money, and he continued to take responsibility for her mother's utility bills too. But he invited her less and less to their hotel room, and when he did it was to massage his back—to ease the tension in his shoulders.

2 THE LANDOWNER'S DAUGHTER

There is more to the truth than just the facts.
~ Author Unknown ~

Davina had always said she grew up poor, ignored, and rejected by her father, the biggest landowner in the district. The only time she remembered her father speaking to her or referring to her was in 1945 when she was ten years old and her mother had sent her to ask him for his help just before Christmas.

Davina and her mother had things from their acreage to eat and chickens to slaughter for meat, but they had no money to buy things from the stores in Spanish Town. Her mother would have liked to have had fabric to make new clothes. It had been a long time since they had had anything new to wear, and they badly needed new shoes.

~~~~~

Davina and her mother Icelyn lived in Edmount, a district four miles from Spanish Town. Edmount was small, even by district standards. Even in Edmount's most populous time, there were never more than thirty families living on its hillsides or in its valleys.

Even though Spanish Town was only a few miles away, the district was light-years away from Spanish Town. The only road through the district was not paved with asphalt; it was a dirt road overridden with potholes. When Davina was a child, there was no electricity and piped-in water was unpredictable, so each household collected water in tanks when it rained.

There were two churches in the district, but there was no school or library. The children of Edmount walked two miles to Saint John's Road for primary school and four miles to Spanish Town for high school.

Davina and the other residents of Edmount considered themselves poor, not because they sought sympathy but rather as a matter of fact. Children grew up knowing that the land was their saviour. They understood that they needed rain to fall (but not too much) and wind to blow (but just enough) in order to live off the land.

They understood too that they needed the favour of the biggest landowner and employer in the district. He and his family before him owned well over half of the land in the district: raising livestock and cultivating coffee, pimento, and cedar. The relationship between the landowner and the residents of the district was uneasy, not because of how he sullied women, because the residents depended upon his vast acreage for their survival. The residents of the district always treaded carefully around the landowner.

The landowner was married to a lady from Kingston. The lady's father owned a big store and had horses that ran in the races. Davina had never seen this lady but had heard that she was very tall and that she and her children wore different clothes every day. Her children did not walk barefoot or carry heavy loads on their heads to sell things in the market alongside their mother like Davina did.

Davina had seen the landlord riding his oversized horse through the district and collecting rents from the tenants. A few times he had ridden past her as she collected water from the standpipe on the road.

~~~~~

Davina was nervous as she approached the big house with the large, iron gate. Standing in front of the house that her mother told her belonged to her father, she couldn't help but wonder, *Does my father know that I am his daughter?*

She had never been to that part of the district—she had had no business there. The location of the big house was beyond the convenience store, well past her church, and not in the direction of her school. Until today, she had never set eyes on the big, iron gates that led to her father's home.

Davina did not know why her mother had decided after all these years to send her to her father at this time. She grew up hearing that he had changed from the days when he had been smitten by her mother. It was no surprise that he had fallen for Davina's mother over all of the other girls in the district, since she had been the shyest, most sheltered, and prettiest girl in the district.

"He has turned into a worthless man," her mother had said, "after tricking me with his sweet words, taking what he wanted, and getting me pregnant." He had nothing more to do with Icelyn after she became pregnant. Davina never heard her mother mention words of romance, love, friendship, or affection in the same breath that she mentioned her father. Whatever it was that occurred between her mother and her father seemed cold and harsh.

As she opened the gate and walked tentatively up the long driveway to the house, she called out, "Please hold the dogs." She passed a gardener, who was sharpening a machete, and a young boy about her age, who was sweeping the yard. The two dogs tethered to trees behind the gardener and the boy did not seem bothered by her. Perhaps they smelled familiar blood.

On the other side of the yard, there was a woman hanging sparkling white sheets on a line with other gleaming white clothes. In the distance behind the clothes lines, Davina spied an oversized chicken coup. She knew they kept other animals too—like horses, cows, pigs, and goats—but only the chickens were near the house.

Davina did not know that houses of that size existed in the world. In Edmount, no one else had a house with more than one floor or one so wide from left to right. Most homes had a veranda, but Davina had never seen a home with a veranda that did not stop at the front of the house but wrapped around the house, embracing the walls. On each side of the upper floor, there was a balcony for viewing the land that seemed to never end. The house was painted her favourite colour, yellow; it made her think of sunshine.

On the veranda, with its red-polished floor, there was an old man sitting in a rocking chair. He looked at her over his reading glasses, lowered the newspaper, and called out: "Maizie, see what this little girl wants." His voice was louder than Davina imagined an old man's voice could be.

Maybe they were used to people coming to beg from them, she thought, especially so near Christmas. "I've come to see my father," Davina said. The old man looked her over but did not change his expression or respond. There was the sound of broom against the wooden floor, but no other sound came from within the house. Davina reasoned that her father's family had already gone to Kingston for the holidays and that the frail, old man had stayed behind to keep company with the helpers and the gardener.

The young woman who answered to the name of Maizie eventually came through one of the doors onto the veranda. "Wey you want, pickney?" she said with rough impatience.

"I've come to see my father." Davina used the pronunciation her mother insisted she use when speaking to adults.

"Gal come afa de people dem property," Maizie shouted.

23

Confused, Davina did not move but looked towards the old man in the rocking chair.

"He can't help you. He's hard of hearing, and I don't want mista to come home and catch you on his land. Go. Leave. Now." Maizie looked her up and down.

Only then did the little Davina remember her bare feet and over worn (though clean) yard clothes. At least her hair was freshly combed—thick, oiled ponytails caressing her ears and the tops of her bare shoulders. Davina played with her ponytails as she turned and walked away.

"You mada should be 'shamed, instead of parading you and sending you here. No one tell her to open her legs to him. Dem breed a women will never learn. Dem open dem legs to so many, they never knew whose chile belong to who. Me no blame him for not owning up to any of dem." Maizie's words haunted Davina.

The gardener and boy followed her with their eyes but did not speak as she walked slowly back to the gate. She was tired and hot; she wished she had asked for water to drink before leaving or rested under one of the shade trees that lined the long driveway. As she approached the gate, she heard the unmistakable sound of horse's hooves. Frightened of the rider not seeing her and being trampled by the horse, she stepped aside.

Her father hesitated only long enough to notice that she was inside, not outside, his gate. "What's this little insect doing inside my gate?" He manoeuvered his horse into a trot and sped away from her and up the drive.

While standing at the gate in disbelief, Davina once again wondered if her father knew that she was his daughter.

Upon returning home, Davina told her mother what had happened at her father's house. Davina and her mother were enraged. Icelyn quarrelled, fussed, and fumed to herself for the rest of the day, repeating again and again aloud and in her head, *Little insect inside my gate.*

The following day, there was no further mention of the matter, and Icelyn borrowed money from neighbours and made a good Christmas for her daughter. Never again did Icelyn expose her daughter to ridicule and insult, never again did she mention *father* to Davina.

~~~~~

Over the years, Davina fantasized about her father; mostly she fantasized about the relationship between him and her mother. She held no hope of ever finding out about their relationship. Was the relationship as cold and unfeeling as her mother seemed to suggest? Did she mean nothing to him as the helper had suggested? Did the relationship only mean something to her mother because of the child it produced? She tried not to judge her mother too harshly.

Life for Davina and Icelyn was unrelentingly hard: yielding produce from a small plot of land, walking eight miles, and spending all day selling produce at the market in Spanish Town. But somehow they managed, and they seldom went to bed hungry.

Her mother was especially satisfied that she had managed to send her to school. Davina could read at age six and went to school until she was eighteen. After high school, Icelyn managed to send her to commercial college. There were days without lunch, months with the same worn-out clothes and shoes, and periods when she had to walk ten miles to and from her college, but she bore these burdens in silence.

While working in a government office as a teenager and young woman, Davina sometimes glimpsed at her father and his children on their occasional visits to Spanish Town. Her father and his children had moved away from the district long ago. They lived mainly in Kingston and only occasionally visited the old house Davina had gone to so many years ago as a child seeking help at Christmas.

The vast acreages of land and the big house sat empty except for the gardener; old, barren Maizie (as the old women in the district referred to her); and the remains and spirits of his deaf, now deceased, father and other departed family members buried behind the house.

When Davina fell in love for the first time, she wondered how the sweetness she felt could ever end—the way it had for her mother. Davina wondered if her mother had ever felt the heat of love from her father: his firm, tender embrace, his warm breath on her face, and the sound of his heart beat while lying in his arms afterwards. Had her mother ever felt the excitement and euphoria of moving in dance-like rhythm, each time more intense than the last? It seemed impossible to Davina that her mother had ever experienced any of that, and it made her indescribably sad.

Whether it was true or not that her mother had only been with her father as her mother had lamented over the years, Davina did not know. To Davina, her mother's lament was the saddest refrain—one she vowed she would never utter.

Davina sought many experiences of love and refused many offers of marriage, experiencing the diversity of sweetness that men had to offer until her early thirties. She would not lament as her mother had: "He was my first and only." Davina marvelled in the revelation that each man could be so wonderfully different, so wonderfully kind. She wished her mother had discovered the sweetness and kindness of men and had not stopped after being with her father.

Davina eventually married; she had four children. She was careful not to have only one child like her mother. She did not want a child of hers to feel the pressure and burden she had felt by being an only child. Her family moved to England in the early sixties, but her mother refused to go with them. Her mother's whole world had centred around seven of the fourteen parishes in Jamaica. Her mother had spent most of her life on an acre of land in the district— an acre that four generations of her family had lived and died on.

Davina returned to Jamaica to bury her mother when she died of an inherited stomach condition in her mid-sixties. She had been physically strong in her body up to the end, although the great disappointment of her life was deeply etched on her face.

After her mother's burial while wandering the district, Davina discovered her father had died some five years earlier and his wife a couple of years after him. Their children had moved abroad, and no one had seen or heard from them since they left Jamaica. Maizie too had died. Only Obadiah (the young man she saw sweeping the yard over thirty years ago) was still alive. He and his wife lived in the gardener's lodge and tended to the old house and land. The big house sat empty, in the futile hope that one of the children or grandchildren might visit.

As she walked the district, Obadiah called to her and told her that she looked the same. They laughed heartily together, sharing nearly eighty years of living between them and the memory of her slight over three decades earlier.

Every few years, Davina travelled back to Jamaica. Ten years after her mother's death their old house finally went down in a storm. Obadiah looked after the acre for her. To prevent the land from turning into a wilderness, he periodically cut and weeded the land. And in their district, where only those with history and connection stayed or wandered through, none of the land needed protecting. Everyone freely picked the fruit that nature provided from all the unoccupied land.

Davina and her husband moved back to Jamaica after they retired, leaving their now grown children in England. Nostalgia might have taken them back to the nearly deserted district where she grew up, but good sense prevailed and they built a house in Spanish Town. Over the years, she visited the district, wandering through the old lanes she loved and sitting on her mother's tombstone with the spirits of her grandparents and great-grandparents around her. As a show of belonging, she did not visit the district without going through the big gate on her father's property. Now with confidence, she sat on her father's property for long periods with Obadiah and his family.

One year while visiting with Obadiah, she heard that a couple of her half-siblings had died since her last visit. The news did not move her in any way. They had not known each other.

"If we had met, they would never have accepted me," she had told him.

He nodded knowingly.

When she was in her seventies, she received a letter from a lawyer whose firm she did not recognise. She asked her husband to read it. The look on his face frightened her. "What happen?" she asked. The thumping in her chest was almost audible.

"It says here that the land in the district belongs to you now. You are the last surviving heir."

"What land? What heir? Surviving what? What district?"

Eventually, she made sense of it. All her siblings had died, and her father's land now belonged to her. Before he died, he had made that wish clear in his will.

All she could say at the time was "I didn't know he counted me, I didn't know I mattered."

She would never come to understood the relationship between her father and mother. Only once in her life was she personally acknowledged by her father—the day he insulted her as she stood at his gate—a memory that haunted her for over sixty years. And now he had named her, above his grandchildren, as his heir.

She went to the district after probate was complete. She sat on her mother's tomb and spoke to her as if she were there in person. "He must have counted and loved you too," she said. She sat there crying tears she did not know she had—crying seventy-five years of unshed tears.

3 SWEET AS YOU ARE

By the time the fool has learned the game,
the players have dispersed.
~ Ashanti Proverb ~

I am waiting at Sangster International Airport in Montego Bay, about to leave Jamaica for good. I am on my way to Canada to join my son and his wife. My plan is to stay with them for a while, find work, and then get a place of my own. I will have to find my own place pretty quick because Cassie, my son's new wife, probably won't want me in her house for very long. I can imagine how my son, Christopher, has had to appeal to her good nature, given what she has recently found out about me. I long for them to have children and for me to be a grandmother. Perhaps when I am a grandmother, Cassie will soften towards me. Children have a way of making people shift their focus.

I catch myself looking around. It is more likely that I will see someone I know while I am at the airport than when I am on the plane, but it is easier to pretend not to notice people on the plane than at the airport. I am at the same location on my e-reader as I was when I sat down at the gate two hours ago.

It is the second time in my life that I find myself running away, leaving behind a mess that I created. I am over forty years old and too old now to bury things. Writing these words is progress for me because until now I have not been able to face the last twenty-five years full-on. How could I?

Sometimes, inexplicably, I feel her presence. Maybe her presence is more palpable to me today because I am, at last, leaving her behind. Today I am feeling the strongest sense of her since the day I found her lifeless body—her warm body with packets of my painkillers by her side and a note slipping from her hand—in the room where she had, in her inimitable ways, opened my eyes to a life I had never known—in the room where we had gossiped, fantasised, dreamed, played, completed homework, and planned for the future, as only girls can do.

I am recalling the day that a confusion (something bigger than either of us could have ever imagined) came into our lives—a muddle brought so close to her that her action was perhaps the most sensible thing she could think to do.

I can still hear her mother's voice and feel the taste of her mother's anger and bitterness in my mouth. For many years, her mother's voice and the look on her mother's face had been blotted from my memory—that is, until today. As I close my eyes and knit my furrowed brow, I'm able to bring her voice to me, draw it into my head, to the forefront of my consciousness, and turn up the volume. Her mother's words now resonating with force: *It is you who should have had the courage to do what she did.*

~~~~~

I think Sandy chose me to be her friend because she felt sorry for me. We met when we were eleven; it was our first day in high school. I was the only one in class with a scholarship from a primary school that none of the other pupils had heard of. All the other students had gone to prep school—a type of school that I had not heard of until that week. I was from rural Saint Andrew, a place that most of the pupils had not heard of and a place that their parents would not take them to visit. The other students were from affluent places in

34

Kingston and Saint Andrew whose names ended with *hill, dale,* or *heights.* Their parents or their chauffeurs drove them to school. I took the bus from the country and then a route taxi to school.

Sandy may have also chosen me because we both had Oriental and Jamaican blood. Later on, people would often ask if we were sisters, but we could not have been less like sisters. Her parents were businesspeople with large shops in downtown Kingston, and they had a last name that most people in Kingston had heard of because their shops had their name on them.

My parents were shopkeepers too, but they only owned a small shop in the rural area of Saint Andrew. We were known in our area because we owned the only shop. We sold everything that people in our area and the surrounding areas needed: groceries, hardware, clothes, and odds and ends. My father picked up goods to sell from the wholesalers in downtown Kingston on his weekly trips to town. My father's truck was one of only a few motor vehicles in our area, and his old truck gave him more trouble than it gave him good service. Sandy's parents had two vehicles: a pickup truck for him and a big car for her.

My parents grew ground provisions; almost every type of fruit and vegetable you could think of grew on our land. People throughout our district and people from districts further away came to buy produce from my parents to resell in their town market. Compared to Sandy's mother, my parents were much older. Both of my parents were also older than Sandy's father, Robert, who was ten years older than his wife, Madge.

My parents had me after years of trying and after years of my mother enduring subtle ribbing that she could not keep the babies she got. People may not have meant her harm, but she took it to heart, my father said. I grew up being called special by my mother and being adored by my father. From the stories I heard, my father did not mind not having children, but he was sad and upset that my mother's womb would not hold the children he gave her.

Sandy's mother, Madge, told me proudly that she had Sandy at seventeen and was not sorry that Providence had not given her any more children.

"My mother loves being younger than my father," Sandy told me once. "She thinks men stay with their wives if they are younger."

I couldn't imagine anyone not wanting to be with Sandy's mother. Her mother was really beautiful, and not just to my young eyes. She was tall and slim with hair that was always shiny and styled. I never saw her wear yard clothes. Whenever I visited after school and even when no one was expected at her home, she was always dressed as if expecting visitors. I saw the way other parents looked at her too. When she picked up Sandy from school, she did not wait in her vehicle like the other parents; she parked and stood at the school gate—like a perfectly drawn picture.

Sandy's father, Robert, did not fuss about his appearance like his wife did. I would never have matched them together, if I had seen them separately on the street. He was much shorter than her and stout with a pale, puckered complexion as compared to her smooth, flawless skin and shapely figure. I could not put it into words back then when I was eleven going on twelve and he was thirty-nine, but now looking back on everything that had happened, I think he got ahead of himself. He had not been in the moment—he was in another time and another place with thoughts outside of what was happening at that time.

On the first day of high school, Sandy came and sat next to me in the dinner hall. She told me that she had been watching me all morning as we went through our orientation: touring the rooms where we would have our lessons, reviewing our timetable with our form teacher, meeting the principal, and being told about responsibilities and expectations.

"Where are you from? I have never seen you anywhere before," she said, looking with a full smile at me.

"I haven't been anywhere before," I replied. I remember feeling foolish because of my country accent and because everyone has been somewhere—even if somewhere is not where other people have been.

"So where did you go to gymnastics and music lessons?"

"We don't have any of those in my district, but I can play tambourine. I play that in church."

Sandy laughed at me, but I didn't mind. She was talking to me, and if other girls were watching, they might think that I had told a joke and made her laugh.

At the end of the day, Sandy made her mother drop me off at the bus stop. When I got home, my mother wanted me to tell her about my first day at the big high school in Kingston. Pride was all over her. I was the only girl from anywhere near where I lived who had passed the Common Entrance to that school. All I wanted to talk about was Sandy: how pretty she was, how nice she was, how lovely she spoke, the big car her mother drove, and the nice clothes her mother wore.

"You are a strange girl," my mother said. "When your father comes you better find something to tell him about what you learnt in school. He won't be happy with talk of a best friend when you hardly been there a minute."

Schoolwork was never a challenge for me. My father wanted me to become a doctor, so I had to put my head into my work, which he told me every day.

"You may have got a scholarship, but we still have to find fare, lunch, school uniform, and book money," he often reminded.

My mother would reprimand him: "Don't put pressure on her. She always does her best. And besides what else would we do with the money we work so hard to make?"

Our house and shop were on land that was left to my father by his mother. The main road to our district was not paved. It was made of stones and marlstone that was easy or arduous for vehicles to manoeuvered over depending upon the amount of rain—but always unforgiving on shoes and bare feet. A lane lead from the main road to the entrance of our three-bedroom board house and separate shop. The shop, which faced the main road, was a simple one-room, rectangular building with a counter running down the middle and stock arranged on shelves or in cabinets behind the counter. Customers called for what they wanted, and my mother or father fetched the items called. Before I started high school, I helped in the shop on Saturdays; but after I started school, my parents said that every spare moment not spent at school or on the four-hour commute had to be spent over my books. It was not that my parents begrudged me some spare time. It was more about me spending so many hours on the bus and taxi going to and from school that I had little time for much else.

Sandy and I grew close. I became the sister she said she wished she had, and she became the sibling I never had. Her mother seemed to like me too, and after the first time her mother invited me home for dinner and to spend the night, I did not have to take the route taxi to get my bus. From that day forward, her mother took me to the bus stop every day after school, so I only had to take the country bus—plus my fifteen-minute walk—to get home.

Sandy often invited me to her home after school, and my parents allowed me to spend an hour at her home doing homework until the days got darker in November.

At her home, she let me try on her clothes; we talked about having periods and prayed that they would come. She said she did not want to be "pretty dunce" like her mother. To me, calling her mother pretty dunce behind her back was tantamount to cursing her in broad daylight in front of a crowd. I told her in whispered tones that she should honour her father and her mother. She laughed and simply said, "Speak the truth and speak it ever; cost it what it will."

"I want a job, my own money, my own life, and then I will marry if I want," she said with certainty. Even then, I wondered how she had come to know (let alone voice) such thoughts.

But Sandy was different in so many ways. When other children laughed at my country accent, ridiculed me for having to ride public transport, and said they had not heard of the place where I lived, she shrugged as if my difference was desirable and wished that others could see that too.

I was ashamed to take her home, but she insisted on spending a weekend over Christmas vacation in the country with me. She knew country life, she had said, because her nana lived on a country estate.

I warned her that we did not live on an estate and about our conditions: piped-in water was unpredictable, there was no asphalted road to our home, we bathed in a big pan in a little room behind our house, and we had mosquitoes as big as flies, sometimes burning cow dung to ward them off. Each dire picture I painted fuelled her interest even more.

"None of that is strange to me," she insisted.

We were both twelve years old when Sandy first stayed with me and my family for a weekend during Christmas vacation; from then on, it was a tradition. Each long vacation—Easter, Christmas, and summer—Sandy packed her bags and her father drove us in his pickup to my home.

Through her eyes, I painted a new and extraordinary picture of my house and the five acres of land upon which it sat. After each holiday, her memories and experiences at my home were the topic of how she had spent her holiday. Because of the wondrous picture she painted, I became the second most popular girl in our class—next to her.

Until Sandy visited, I had never considered the fireflies, which flashed their lights in the trees around our house, magical; the woodpeckers, owls, and hummingbirds amazing; the lizards anything but worrisome; or the countless fruits and vegetables (which grew lavishly on our land) wondrous. Through her eyes, my humble home became a place worthy of end-of-vacation stories. She even noticed and glorified the old men as they walked home from the fields with a load of firewood or ground provisions upon their heads and the hampered donkeys as they bore their loads.

The area children were sure that the blind woman up the road from our house was an Obeah woman. The woman terrified me because of the fantastical stories the children in the area made up about her. The woman called out to us when Sandy was around, and Sandy confidently strutted up her lane with me trembling behind her. At the young age of twelve and over the years, Sandy spent time with the woman asking the woman questions about her childhood and hearing stories about how she laboured like a mule to keep her family alive. "You are too ahead of this time," the woman once told Sandy. "You may have to go and come." I did not know what she meant. When she spoke, she turned to us as if her blind eyes could see. "Some people leave this life early and are reborn again," she had said, with a laugh that could have been a grunt.

"She frightens me," I told Sandy, after we left. "I don't want to go back. When she speaks like that, I feel cold, and the hairs on my arms stand up."

"Me too," Sandy said with gleaming eyes. "But I like it."

In my second year of high school, my parents discussed boarding me in Kingston. They said that the four-hour, daily round-trip was taking a toll on my health. I was not sure why they thought I was unhealthy; I was never sick and had not complained. My mother took me through the usual "wash-out" routine (an infusion of the foulest tasting garden herbs and barks) at the start of each and every holiday. I had to drink the awful infusion before bed each night for a week if it was a long holiday or for a weekend if it was a short holiday. Take it from me, I was washed out. During those days, I was never far from our latrine. I always had a termly visit to the doctor, and apart from the usual diatribe by my mother that I was too thin (even though I ate like a horse), all seemed to be officially well with my health.

We visited a few potential families who lived within a short taxi ride from the school and offered to board high school students, but those closest to the school were too expensive for us. When Sandy heard about our search, she asked her parents if I could board with them during the weekdays, going home on the weekends. Sandy told me that her father was more hesitant than her mother, but eventually Sandy persuaded them.

There were several spare rooms, but Sandy insisted that I take the room adjoining her room, which was her study and private sitting room at the time.

I instinctively took to calling her parents Uncle Robert and Aunt Madge, instead of addressing them as mister and misses.

Even though we had our own rooms, Sandy and I spent more and more time sharing a room and rarely slept in a room alone. Her mother said we were more like sisters than real sisters usually were. Her parents refused to take cash from my parents, settling instead for ground provisions from our land that my father dropped off on his way to the wholesalers in downtown Kingston. In the summer months, the ground provisions were very plentiful, especially the mangoes, avocados, and tangerines. At other times of the year, callaloo, cabbage, and onions were plentiful. Madge would say, "The taste of the produce from that district is better than anything I buy in town." As an afterthought, she would add, "It's hard to believe that Robert's people have thousands of acres in that district lying there producing almost nothing."

"People from my district sell in the Coronation Market too," I told her. I was proud that produce from my humble area found its way to the most famous market on the island.

"It must be your father's particular ground then," she insisted. "There is a special taste to the food that comes from his land."

It made me happy that she liked what we had to offer in payment for their kindness towards me.

I cannot remember the exact time when Robert began to drive me within walking distance of my home on Fridays or when it became his habit. Madge always took me to the bus stop, so I did not have to take the taxi. One evening after she had driven away, Robert drove up in his truck. I was surprised to see him. He said he was going to visit a friend in the hills of Saint Andrew and could drop me at the crossroad where the main road met the lane leaving me my fifteen-minute walk home. I understood why he did not want to take me all the way home: the lane was difficult and unpaved, and the good road continued in the direction towards where he said his friend lived.

Sandy and I grew closer over the years. We were not the kind of best friends who divulged secrets or chatted about nothing. We were the kind of best friends who understood and helped each other when a subject challenged one friend but was easy for the other. We listened to each other's complaints about teachers and parents, and we each understood what made the other one cry, sad, or happy.

We started our periods two months apart—me first, then her. During my first period, I had no pain. When I got my period the second time, I threw up repeatedly and the pain was so intense that I could not go to school; I even fainted a couple of times. Sandy never had any pain, but she understood and took over caring for me from the housekeeper Betty when she came home from school. I did not need much looking after because I could not keep food down and because I needed to be alone with my cries and groans. Betty would make me a flask of cold drinks and another of hot tea and leave them in my room. She would leave a packet of hard crackers because I was not allowed to take my pills (every four hours) without food. On that one day of every month, I sometimes wished I would die.

Until Robert started driving me home on Fridays, I did not think that he had noticed me around his home. He often came home late from work and spent his evenings with Madge in their room or in the sitting room they kept for themselves. Once or twice when he came into the family sitting room where Sandy and I would watch TV, he simply said, "I hope you girls are working hard at your schoolwork." Sandy would jump to hug and kiss him. He would smile at me and then leave us to our own devices.

We spent most of our time in either Sandy's room or my room, and he did not venture down that hallway when I was there.

Their two-story home was located on one of the famed hills in Saint Andrew. The bedrooms were all located on the second floor, and the second floor had two hallways running parallel to each other with a large opening between the hallways that afforded a view of the sunken sitting room below. Each hallway was described by the name of the family member whose bedroom was at the end of that hallway. Sandy's hall was so named because it led to Sandy's room, my room (her old sitting room), and two guestrooms. Madge's hall led to three rooms shared by the couple: a study, a sitting room, and a bedroom. On the ground floor, there were three other rooms plus the kitchen and dining room. One of the other rooms on the first floor was Robert's special room where he entertained his friends: drank, played dominoes, and watched cricket when there was a Test Match. He also supported Arsenal, a team in the Premier League of English football.

It surprised me that a grown man could be so devoted to a football team to let winning and losing affect his mood.

When Sandy showed me Robert's special room, she said, "You can go anywhere downstairs apart from this room. Daddy doesn't even let the housekeepers clean it unless he is in there. I often go in it though when he is not here. When I was little, he used to let me sit with him and watch cricket or football if he didn't have friends over. He taught me the rules of cricket so early I can't remember not knowing them. As for football, I even understand the offside rule."

"What rule?" I asked.

"Boring. You won't want to know."

Robert's special room was a large room arranged as a bedroom and sitting room in one. There was a double bed in one corner, partially hidden by a huge, decorative wooden screen with four sections connected by brass hinges. In the rest of the expansive room, there were several armchairs, a three-seater sofa, a table (with several domino sets in decorative boxes) and chairs, a liquor cabinet, and a gigantic TV on the wall.

Outside and at the back of the property stood a house for the two live-in housekeepers and an adjoined, but separate, one-room, self-contained apartment for the gardener. There was always somewhere to hide or be private, in their home.

Our conversation was stilted when Robert drove me partway home on the first Friday. I did not feel terribly uncomfortable with him, but I was not sure how I was expected to behave—especially since he asked me not to mention to anyone in the family that he had driven me. Because his tone had been so relaxed, I thought that maybe it did not matter whether I told or not. As soon as I got home, I told my mother that he had given me a ride and what he had said.

"He must have a sweetheart in these parts," she said. "Those men always have a countrywoman as a sweetheart. They want to do their badness away from their fine ladies from town. I don't like that he is making you a part of that dirtiness."

My mother's annoyance made me uneasy, but she was right. I kept no secrets from Sandy, so it would be hard not to tell her, and more than that I did not want to be the cause of any trouble between Robert and Madge. I decided to keep my mouth shut.

As the months passed, I became more comfortable and at ease with Robert. He would ask me about myself: what I liked in school, what I liked to do in my spare time, and what I wanted to do when I finished school. He spoke like a father or real uncle would, asking questions and only distantly interested in the answers. We chatted easily about a wide variety of topics: school, Sandy, our district, and my future plans. He was the only adult I knew who did not speak to me as if I was a child. When I was with him, I was a person like anyone else; in turn, the more time I spent with him on our drives the more mature I felt. So much so that it was hard to be a teenager again when I returned home, and even harder when I visited his family's home where I had to put distance and unfamiliarity between us.

One day when he switched our conversation to whether I had a boyfriend, I thought he was asking me, in a roundabout way, to spy on Sandy. Of course, there was nothing to lie about because neither of us was seeing anyone at the time. Sandy and I received more than our fair share of attention from boys. We laughed at most of their childish ways, although we fantasised together about dating when we turned sixteen.

In between our Friday trips, I caught myself thinking about what Robert and I would talk about on the next journey. On Friday afternoons, I found myself making a special effort tidying my hair and clothing in the bathroom before meeting Madge who took me to the bus stop—and to Robert.

I can't remember the exact time when I stopped seeing Robert as an old man or as my best friend's father or as the short man who was twenty-seven years older than me. All I knew was that he was so different from the skinny boys who called to me on the road or waylaid us after school—the boys with their dirty jokes and pretence who didn't know what they were talking about.

When Robert walked, he walked like he knew where he was going; when he talked, like he knew what he was saying; and when he listened to you, like he understood. When he sat down, he controlled that space. Even before my sixteenth birthday, I wanted to be in his company.

In the days leading up to Friday as I struggled to keep my thoughts about him to myself, I longed for the drive through the hills of Saint Andrew but dreaded the painful crossroad where he would stop to let me out. Then as I walked slowly home, I'd wish we were not in a situation where we had to hide and be secretive.

Throughout the year that I was fifteen and Robert drove me home on Fridays, our intimacy was mainly in my head and in my dreams. No one could have accused him of behaving improperly towards me.

He drove, and we talked; he asked me questions, and I answered.

One evening he hugged me after he stopped to let me out. My whole body burnt as never before, as I had never thought possible. I was not afraid of my body like most girls my age. I had explored my body, enjoying private moments and bringing about my physical peaks. But the first time Robert hugged me was like all of those times of bringing myself to crests of enjoyment rolled into one and then some more. It amazed me that a simple hug could charge every nerve in my body.

I was close to my mother, so I was not surprised when she noticed that I was at times absentminded and pensive. "You not getting yourself mixed up with a boyfriend," she had accused. "You are not sixteen yet, and boyfriends are not for school girls."

My father was more relaxed than my mother about my coming of age, as he called it. "Jean is a sensible child. Older than her age, has always been. She is not going to fool around with little juvenile boys. She's going to college," he had stated with pride, as if I were already in college. "You'll be the first girl from our little district and in our family to achieve such a feat."

Sandy and I, along with a couple of other girls in our year group, had taken our Ordinary Level courses one year early. We were now one year ahead and taking Advanced Level courses. Having achieved all As in my O-Levels, papa spoke of his ambitions for me with confidence.

A few months after Robert gave me the first hug, he changed our routine. One day he told me to not wait at the bus stop but to wait at a nearby shop a little way off. From that point on, he changed the meeting place each week and secretly told me where to meet. It amazed me how he communicated to me without Sandy, Madge, two housekeepers, or the gardener suspecting that we had anything to do with each other outside their home.

After the initial worry about being deceptive and shutting out my best friend, I found myself excited by the idea that no one knew about my private life with Robert—not even my dearest friend, Sandy.

At our rendezvous as soon as Robert pulled up in his truck, I slipped into the passenger seat beside him in a second.

In character, Robert was always calm and attentive. When we were together and as soon as I entered his space, his whole focus was on me. He was never over effusive. As I got to know him, I understood why Madge had fallen for him when she was young and why he had fallen for a woman ten years his junior. There was a calm that surrounded him and drew you in, enveloping you with a feeling of safety and warmth. He did not throw himself at me like boys my age wanted to do; he was not rapacious or predatory. He settled in his space and watched as his energy drew you to him. This was how I felt on one particular Friday.

As I moved to get out of the truck on this particular Friday, I felt his eyes and turned. He was looking intently at me with an almost imperceptible smile. I gravitated towards his arms and rested there for a few moments. At first, I felt my arms tighten around his neck; then I felt his arms tighten around my waist. We held each other. A feeling of warmth spread through my body: it seemed like the air conditioner had been turned off and the midday sun was descending all its force upon me. His cheeks were soft, not bristly like my father's, whose unshaven face was the only experience I had had of a man's face against mine. He pulled away, slipping his hand into mine, and then kissed the back of my hand repeatedly. Gently he pulled me to him again. I turned so that our lips could meet. But he averted his face, and my lips brushed against his cheek. He seemed to rearrange himself in the seat before he let me go.

"Have a good weekend," he said. "Keep as sweet as you are."

Those words rang in my head the whole weekend. I did not know how I could last two days without seeing him.

In the following week, I did not see Robert at all. I was convinced that he was avoiding me. During almost every passing second, the thought of asking Sandy where her father was lingered on the tip of my tongue.

A month or so earlier, Sandy had said without ado that one of the girls from school had seen me in her father's truck. "I suppose he was going to Nana's," she had said. She proceeded to tell me that her father had been brought up in Saint Mary, one of the parishes adjacent to Saint Andrew where I lived, and that he drove near where I lived to get there. For the first time since the private journeys had begun, I felt at ease and almost relieved about the idea that he did not have a country mistress as my mother had thought.

When we turned sixteen, Sandy planned a joint party for us at her home. I was excited about the party and reaching sweet sixteen, as Robert called it. Robert was in the house on the day of the party. He came laden with gifts for his daughter and a small packet for me. My gift was a gold bracelet, which upon close examination bore inside the words *Stay as Sweet as You Are*. It was hard to disguise my happiness and relief.

One morning as we ate breakfast before school, Sandy asked, "Is something the matter with you? You are quiet these days as if you are somewhere else. What's wrong?"

I didn't get the chance to answer because the sound of raised voices thundered into the room. It was Robert and Madge. In all the years that I had boarded with them, I had never heard a row in the house like that. Irritated, impatient words, yes—but never at the decibel that had just shaken the house. Sandy commented disinterestedly that her mother thought Robert was having an affair.

"Not sure why she tells me these things. I'm not her sister. I don't want to know. She reckons she can tell me anything. You should know. My dad was engaged to be married to someone else when my mother got pregnant with me. I love my dad, but…."

She did not finish because the row moved from upstairs to the front door as Madge followed him with her accusing words. Robert was now silent. I heard him slam the door of his truck, start the engine, and drive away.

My heart was racing. I tried to make myself small at the dining table. I was afraid: if Madge heard my thumping heart, she would turn accusing looks at me and ask me to silence the beat of my heart.

Does she suspect me? Does the family know that every moment I am in their home—whether he is in the house or not—I am overwhelmed by his presence or by my memories of him?

If we crossed on the upstairs landing, accidentally met in the kitchen, or gathered on the wraparound veranda, I was tortured by the emotions that bubbled through me. I fought to keep my eyes from wandering towards him. I feared that one day, forgetting where I was, I would blurt out something giving myself away or do something foolish like reach out and take his hand or turn and hug him. I understood he could not pay me any attention, but I still longed for a glance. I wanted to know if he too pined for our next slow drive into the hills.

We left for school shortly after Robert had stormed away. "Are you on your period?" Sandy said, as Madge turned out of the drive. "You haven't been looking well."

"I'm fine," I said, hoping she would stop talking.

Madge's silence was palpable. I longed to be away from them and in the refuge of my classroom.

The house was back to its calm quiet that evening. I did not see Madge after she took us home from school, and I did not hear or see Robert for the rest of the week.

Robert was especially attentive and warm to me the Friday after the row. His soft melodious voice enveloped me as I slid into the car. "You look sweet," he said. I smiled and sat with my hands between my knees. I was shivering. "Is the air conditioner too cold? I can turn it down, or open the window when we get out of the town."

"I'm not cold," I said.

He felt behind his seat and brought out a bag with soft drinks and snacks. Each week he brought drinks, and he varied the snacks: from peanuts, crackers and cheese, bun and cheese, to sliced fruit in a covered plastic container. I was not hungry.

"You mustn't worry about Madge and me, you know. We have our problems. No one is the cause of them but me and her."

He reached across and took my hand. I always liked the way he was able to drive with one hand. How he could focus on the road, turn to me with his penetrating eyes momentarily, and then return his gaze to the road—evading potholds, negotiating steep bends, and avoiding precipices.

"I won't let anything happen to you," he said, squeezing my hand. Then he raised my hand to his lips and kissed it repeatedly.

My parents were not expecting me to come home on one particular weekend. The week before this particular weekend, Robert had suggested that I tell them I had a test and needed to stay over in Kingston to study—as I sometimes did. He told me to take some clothes from his house, to make it look like I was going home.

We drove to his family's home in Saint Mary where he was brought up. His father had died a few years back, and his mother was abroad helping his sister with her children. Their home was on over two thousand acres and had been part of a sugar estate. The great house had long fallen down, he reported. His childhood home had been the estate overseer's house.

"Thank goodness, my family is not from a line of dastardly slave owners," he said, as he manoeuvered his truck along the long driveway lined with pink and white bougainvillea.

The driveway to the carport and house was so long that you could not see the buildings from the road. The main house was a Georgian mansion with a stone base and a plastered upper story. It was set on an incline with a panoramic view of hills, valleys, and the Caribbean Sea in the distance.

Robert pulled up in front of the house. There were six steps leading up to gigantic double doors made of local cedar. The doors opened into a hall that had a polished wooden floor like the rest of the house. The study, sitting room, powder room, and several bedrooms were on that floor. The rooms were all neat and tidy, like pictures of how properly kept rooms should look, but they were lifeless as if no one had used them properly for years.

The house was set on an elevation; the kitchen and dining room were downstairs from the main level. The dining room had a table with at least twelve chairs around it. He told me there were various other rooms on this floor that had belonged to him and his sister: a playroom, a library, and a sitting room. The self-contained servants' quarters were down there too.

And just like his home in town, there were two live-in housekeepers and a live-in groundsman as he called him. He said his mother employed various other dayworkers to look after their livestock and horses. I found it hard to visualize two thousand acres but knew from my parents' five acres that it would take a lot of work to maintain. Several black Doberman pinschers roamed the grounds near the house. I was apprehensive about them. But Robert was right: they did not find me a threat and were keener to show him how much they had missed him.

I asked Robert if Sandy and Madge visited often. "Madge and my mother have never seen eye to eye," he said. "To me, it is my perfect getaway, and it suits me that she likes to stay in town. Sandy comes up when her nana is here."

I suddenly felt embarrassed when the housekeepers came to welcome us with iced drinks. I felt like the young girl that I was. The older of the two women, Mrs. Maxwell, worked hard to avoid my eyes. The younger one, Blossom, wore an unreadable blank expression.

I had gone along with Robert as if spending time with him at his childhood home was the most natural thing in the world. It wasn't until much later in my life that I wondered how I could have done such a thing as a young girl of sixteen. Why hadn't I felt a prick of conscience at that time? Why had I chosen to became an accomplished liar, particularly to my parents and my best friend?

Robert showed me to one of the bedrooms on the top floor and suggested I shower and change. It was only as I undressed for the shower that I lost my nerve. *What am I doing here? What do the housekeepers think of me?*

Blossom had to call me repeatedly when dinner was served. More than once I thought of asking Robert to take me back—but back to where? It was getting late, and I could not go back home, and I certainly could not go back to his home in Kingston.

We ate dinner on the upper veranda: beef soup with root vegetables. All the ingredients came from his estate, even the beef. When we arrived, the unending shades of green hills and valleys and the glimpse of the sea in the distance had given me a sense of security, reminding me of my district. Now this place was shrouded in an unfamiliar darkness: a dark amethyst that made me shiver. The thought of being alone and helpless in unfamiliar surroundings and with people I did not know frightened me.

As darkness fell, the groundsman lit fires to ward off mosquitos. The glow of the fires in the yard below lifted my unease, and I began to relax again.

Mrs. Maxwell and Blossom expertly cleared away the soup bowls and offered ice cream. I looked across the table at Robert. He smiled approval.

After I finished my ice cream, Robert took my hand and led me outside. There were several chairs dotted around the garden. There were chairs swinging from trees, chairs resting casually against garden walls, and others fixed solidly in groups around concrete tables. Robert led us to two chairs that were hanging from a cotton tree furthest away from the house. We sat there talking and drinking from the pitcher of cold drinks the servants had left. I dozed and woke with him watching me and smiling. "Do you feel at home, my sweetness? Are you okay?"

I nodded.

"Feel free to go to bed when you are ready," he said. "I have some old friends coming over later to play dominoes. We have this bad habit when I come up: we drink rum and play dominoes till late. If you need anything, you can always call one of the helpers. But they would have put ice water in your room already."

Surprised, I got up to leave. He stood and took me in his arms. His embrace was firm and protracted. This time, he moved his mouth to mine, and we pressed our lips together.

"Good night," he said. "I will teach you to ride a horse tomorrow.

We have a lot of horses. There is one called Polly; you will like her. She is a gentle soul. Just like you. Good night, my sweet."

I slept soundly; then I awoke in the middle of the night to the sounds of voices talking and laughing and of dominoes slamming on a wooden table on the lower veranda. I fell quickly back to sleep.

I was up at my usual time: six o'clock. Tea was placed on the table soon after I sat down on the veranda. Mrs. Maxwell was sweeping and gave no indication that she noticed me. Blossom asked me whether I wanted to eat or wait for Mr. Robert. "Him always wake late on a Saturday, so you may want to eat before him come out."

I took her suggestion and said I would not wait for him.

After breakfast, I was glad for some time to do my homework. It was well into the afternoon before Robert appeared.

"You studying? Good," he said. He was in his night shorts and a t-shirt.

"I'm finished now," I told him.

My confusion about the night before had now abated. I was relieved and happy that he had given me time to myself. My love and respect for him had increased, and I longed to show him how I felt. After he ate, we drove through the accessible parts of the estate. I enjoyed my first riding lesson with Polly. I told him that riding a horse was not much different than riding a donkey: only the horse was higher and had more personality. He thought that was funny and laughed long and loudly.

"Next time you come, I'm going to teach you to drive," he said.

I laughed with excitement. "I am going to be able to drive a car and ride a horse. I wish I could tell Sandy, but I know I can't," I said hastily.

He did not comment. He knew I understood the unspoken rules.

After dinner, we sat under the cotton tree for a few minutes. He had not said much over dinner and was even quieter as we sat under the moonlit skies. I was lost in my thoughts when he got up, came over, and scooped me up in his arms. He carried me like a baby through the garden, up the steps, past my room, and into his room where he placed me gently on the bed. He stood watching me for what seemed like minutes before he knelt beside the bed and slowly began to slip off my clothes.

We slept together that night. He held me afterwards: silently but repeatedly kissing and stroking my face and neck.

In the weeks that followed, the time we spent together was a blur.

The only constant was how few words he spoke. He never shrouded our closeness with explanations or promises. I sometimes longed for explanations and promises and cried many nights out of fear, rage, and jealousy. But I always woke up knowing that I had to understand and keep everything to myself.

My mother suggested I had changed, and Sandy thought we were growing apart. Sandy was dating, and she wondered why I was not dating since boys were often asking me out. I used my studies as an excuse.

"Funny. You always walk the exams. I am the one who needs to study hard."

One weekend, my father called me out of earshot of my mother and said someone he knew had seen me in a truck with a man in Saint Mary. Lies and untruths had become a part of my life over the past three months, and now one more lie tripped off my tongue about the family taking me to Saint Mary.

"I went to Saint Mary," I said. "Mr. Robert's mother had taken ill, and they were all going and didn't want to leave me alone in Kingston."

"Your mother is worrying about you, Jean. Take care you are not doing anything stupid," said my father.

It was on a Tuesday that everything collapsed around me. I had not seen Robert for a whole week, and he had not been able to take me to Saint Mary or drive me to the crossroads. In my presence around the house, he had been playful, jolly, and unusually chatty with Madge. For some reason, I began to wonder whether he had found someone else. His closeness with Madge bothered me but not as much as the thought of him fancying some other young girl. I longed to know if someone else had caught his eye, but there was no one I could ask. I used all my willpower to not take a taxi to his shop downtown, to not wait up for him at their home, to not follow him around the house, and to not tell everyone what we were doing. But the sensible side of me knew that I had to be patient and wait. But wait for what? I did not know.

During the six months we were together, I did not think that the way I behaved around him in the house had changed. I had perfected *Good morning, Uncle Robert* and *Evening, Uncle Robert*. In the house, I never fully looked at him.

I heard him in the kitchen on one particular Monday morning. I hastily scribbled a note, and in a second as I brushed past him, I pressed it in his hand. *Please come back home tomorrow. I will say I have period pains. I need you. Please.*

It was about the time for my period so Madge or Sandy didn't suspect a thing. The following day Madge gave me a packet of painkillers. I took them to my room, even though I had enough in my stash to last several months. The tablets never helped but had become a habit. I took them when the pains came, swapping and changing brands hoping that one day one of the brands would ease the pain.

It was not that way for Sandy. She did not have bad pains with her period.

Sandy and I had grown apart. She was often preoccupied with her boyfriend and about the ups and downs of dating—almost every conversation was about boys. It began to irritate me, especially since I could not speak about the person I was dating.

Usually somewhere in the conversation she would say, "I am not ready to go further with him yet. My nana has always said, 'You have to be the one who decides, not the boy.' I have decided. I am not ready." She said these words as if she deserved a medal.

I wanted to tell her that she did not know what she was talking about and that it would be her body that would tell her when she was ready, not her mind. But how could I? I was sorry about not being able to tell her that when the time was right it would be like drifting slowly out from the beach, going so far out of your depths with a man that there was no option but to hold on to him so that you could be kept safe. I wanted to say that being with a man, sitting by his side, having him reach out to take and squeeze your hands, and having him take you into his certain arms and hold you was like being out in the deep but still safe and protected. I wanted to tell her that if you talk about whether it is the right time or not then you are still too immature.

The day everything collapsed was a day when Madge's Orchid Society group met. Usually on a day when they met, Madge did not return home after dropping us off at school but would be out all day and pick us up from school before she returned home. Occasionally, if the Orchid Society had an evening event then one of her friends would bring us home after school, and she would return home later.

I showered, dressed in a fresh, clean nightdress, and then got back into bed to wait expectantly for Robert. I was ecstatic when his car drove up outside the house not long after Madge left with Sandy.

I pulled my door ajar and listened to him talking to the housekeepers. I imagined he was giving instructions: to get them out of the main house. Some minutes later, I heard him in Sandy's hallway and then a gentle tap on my door. I put the book I was reading beside me on the bed.

"Come down to my den," he said, from outside the room.

I put on my dressing gown and hurried out of the room, grabbing my novel as I went.

He was smiling and relaxed when I got to his room.

"Are you planning to read to me?" he said, looking at my book.

"Absentminded me. Not sure why I brought it."

"Let me take a shower."

I sat on the covered toilet and watched him. Occasionally, he looked at me and smiled. When he finished, I took the towel, rubbed his body, pushed him gently on the bed, and then straddled him.

"You have magic hands," he said, as I smoothed cream over his back, bottom, and thighs.

"Turn over," I said.

"You will laugh at me. You know I can't control myself when I am near you and sometimes even when I am nowhere near you, my sweet," he said, smiling broadly.

"Do you want to now?" I asked. "I am more than ready," I said, taking his hand to me.

"No, it is sweeter for me the longer I can hold myself. Let me just hold you here for a while."

I relaxed on his outstretched arms.

I no longer focusing on things that did not matter: like his big stomach, that I was much taller than him, or that he was around my father's age. Sometimes out of panic or fear, I tried hard to look at boys my age and will myself to like them and go on dates with them, but I could find anything in them for me and nothing in my heart for them.

"Let me take off your pretty little nightdress," he said, pulling away his hand and taking the nightdress over my head.

"Do you like it?" I smiled playfully.

"I like the way you look in it," he said, "but I like the way you look without it even more."

We were on top of the sheets. His leg moved and touched the book I had brought down from my room.

"What are you reading?"

"*The Fire Next Time.*"

"Interesting title. What is it about?" he asked, pressing his lips against my ear.

"A lot of things," I said.

"Read a bit to me."

I read, "Love takes off the masks that we fear we cannot live without and know we cannot live within. *Love* is not used merely in the personal sense as a state of being or a state of grace, not in the infantile American sense of being made happy, but in the tough and universal sense of quest and daring and growth."

"Love is quest and daring and growth. I like that," he said. "I like that very much. Love is daring and growth. Do you believe that? Tell me what you think."

I frowned. His question made me feel as if I were back in a literature class. I was surprised that he had views on literature and love too, and he asked me to lend him the book when I finished it.

"James Baldwin is one of my favourite writers," I said.

"I read too," he said. "Not as much as I would like, but it is a love of mine, especially cricketers' biographies."

It suddenly occurred to me that we had not spoken much in our stolen and borrowed time. It made me long for more borrowed time and fear the time when it would have to end.

We had not made love yet. He had never given me the impression that it was all about physical intimacy. Times leading up to our lovemaking were always unhurried and special—another thing I adored about him.

The book by James Baldwin was now on the bedside table, and I was lying in his arms with my eyes closed. Then I heard "Oh my God! What are you doing home?"

I thought for a strange moment that he was talking to me. But a silence I had never experienced descended like a shadow at sunset. I opened my eyes and saw Sandy at the opened door.

"Oh my God."

I jumped out of the bed and rushed to her. "Sandy, Sandy."

Sandy did not move or speak. She was looking not at me but at her father who had sat up with the sheet pulled to him.

"Sandy, leave the room. Go! Leave my room now," he ordered.

Sandy did not move. I started to cry. I wanted to cover up, but my legs would not move.

With the sheet still in front of him, Robert got out of the bed,

"Go," he said and he gently moved his daughter out of the room and closed the door behind her.

Robert dressed hurriedly, squeezed my hand, and then followed Sandy out of the room. I heard him calling out to her as he climbed the steps to her room. I dressed, rushed out behind him, and then went to my room. I sat on my bed. I heard Robert in the room next door with Sandy. I heard her wailing—a sound so deep and desperate it could have been from someone immersed in hot oil.

One of the housekeepers had come back into the house. I heard the housekeeper knock on Sandy's door wanting to know what was wrong with her.

I heard Robert's voice. "You can go back to your work. Miss Sandy will be alright." When the housekeeper did not move, Robert repeated the order. "I said, you can go. In fact, go to your quarters until I call you." I heard her hesitant footsteps as she retreated through the hall.

I did not know until that day that anyone could cry for so long and so hard. Eventually, Robert came into my room. "This is not what I wanted. I will have to go and meet Madge. I think I will take her somewhere, so she doesn't come home to this now. I don't know how you are going to do it, but try with Sandy. Try to calm her, until I come back. Make her promise to keep it from her mother until I have time to think." He held me. "Be calm, my sweet. I will fix everything. I will not let anything happen to you."

I heard him drive away. I called to Sandy and tried to go through the adjoining door, but it was locked. I heard the key turn in the door that led to the hall. I called her, begged her to let me in. I called out again and again, but she did not answer. Periodically, I heard her sobbing.

"Sandy, please let me in. I am sorry. Please let me in. It is not Robert's fault. It's mine. Please, just let me say sorry to your face, and then I will leave and go home."

I do not know how long I pleaded with her. Not knowing what to do, I went downstairs and sat in the dining room. The housekeepers were both in the kitchen now shuffling around wanting to know what was going on with Miss Sandy.

"Take some water up to her," one of them said to me, pouring water from the fridge into a glass.

No sound now came from her room. I tried the door to the hall, but the door was still locked. I went into my room and found the adjoining door fully open. She was lying on the bed.

"Oh, Sandy…" I went into her room. It was then that I noticed the empty packets of pills strewn around her lifeless body and a note slipping from her hand. There was a small puddle of water on the floor, and my water flask was lying on its side next to the puddle.

I grabbed the note and slipped it into my school bag. The housekeepers heard my screams and rushed upstairs. The rest of the day was a blur—just flashing images of police cars (car after car, coming and going), school friends coming and going, and the doctor prescribing me pills. But more than all of that, there was Madge's confused weeping and Robert's tears.

No one understood. Everyone focused on me, commenting and questioning: "You were her best friend… Did she tell you anything? Was there boyfriend trouble? Why did she come home from school? What did she say? Where were you when she took the pills?"

As the day went by, the housekeepers added their bits. They had heard her crying and had seen Mr. Robert trying to comfort her. As the questions turned towards Robert, he knew nothing either, so he said.

Robert sent word to my parents. They came and mourned with

the family and added to the list of questions being thrown at me before finally taking me home.

When I got home, I finally read the note. *Why? Jean, how could you and Daddy do that to my mother and me? How could you do that to yourself?*

Over the following week, the questions went on and on, and Robert and I kept silent about the part we had played.

I never went back to school. And not because the story was being pieced together little by little, but because soon after Sandy's funeral, I found out I was pregnant. People around my area began to whisper about me being seen in his truck and that he had often taken me to Saint Mary without his family.

Now that I was pregnant, there was no denying it to my parents. They were completely broken. My father closed the shop for weeks, and my mother hid with me in our yard.

Weeks after the funeral I received a letter from Robert. He could not see me for a while it said. I was numb and did not care. He wrote me again asking when I was going back to school. I did not respond.

When I was six months pregnant and Sandy dead for five months, a car turned into our land. As I looked out, I saw Madge and one of her housekeepers walk from the lane to our house. She had found our district. She had found me and proof of what she had been hearing. I would have run away if I could. My father was in the field; my mother held out her hands to Madge as if to hold her. Madge shook her head. "Your child should have the courage to do what my daughter did." She had driven from town, through the hills and unmade roads to tell me that. I was inconsolable with pain and shame. My mother begged me to pull myself together. She said, if I did not stop my weeping, I would lose the child or give birth to a damaged child.

Robert did not know until Madge's visit that I was pregnant. He came a few days after her visit. My mother stared at him but said nothing. My father called him a dangerous man who should be locked up. We talked, away from my parents.

"Pack everything. You need to be away from all this criticism."

Relieved and happy to see him, I asked him to give me time to talk to my parents.

My mother wanted me to stay at home. "Home with your family is the best place for you. You will need a lot of help through this pregnancy. I was not as lucky as you to get a baby so easily. You can't let the baby suffer. It is not its fault."

My father raged, "It's gone bad already, but you could make it worse by staying in it. The man has a wife. What does he want—a concubine too? I should report him to the police. They should lock him up."

Much later, my mother accused him of having trained me. Much later too, I read about how men groomed young girls by luring and entangling them, but I could not bring myself to accept that was how it went between us.

Hard as it was, I decided to leave the district and my parents' home. My mother wept bitterly. "I'm not leaving the country, Mama," I consoled.

Robert took me to his home in Saint Mary. As we drove through the hills, he said gently, "Why didn't you tell me that you are carrying our child?"

"How could I?" I started to cry.

He allowed me to cry; without speaking, he held and squeezed my hand as he drove.

"You are not the one who is responsible. I take full responsibility. But we have our child to think of now. I will always mourn my dear Sandy, but I have our child to think of now."

Later that week I gave him the note. I watched as he slumped to the floor and wept. Later, he praised my quick thinking in taking the note away.

Years later I found out that he had kept the note, other possessions of his daughter, and the book I was reading that day, Baldwin's *The Fire Next Time*, in a box.

Madge left him after she returned from seeing me pregnant. He said he did not have the strength to beg her to stay. "I could not stand to look into her accusing eyes, so it was all for the best," he had said. Madge got the house in Kingston, and they sold and divided the proceeds of their businesses.

Robert's mother returned to Jamaica when Christopher was a year old and devoted her time to her grandchild. And truth be told, she mainly raised him in those formative years. I happily spent my days riding horses through the estate and hiding in the world of novels: one after another, I bought, borrowed, and devoured books. She and I tolerated each other. I was not happy living in her space, and she only tolerated me for the sake of her beloved grandchild and her son.

Robert and I moved away to Montego Bay when Christopher was five, and we got married the same year. Being in a neutral place improved my mood, but Sandy remained between us despite our outward show. Over the years, I knew that Robert wandered from one woman to the next. I am not ashamed to say that I had my fair share of dalliances too. A few times after we married and when Christopher was away at boarding school, I left Robert and went back to live with my parents in the country. But I always went back, if only to be close to the one thing we had in common—the memory of Sandy.

He was not a bad husband during the twenty years we remained married, but we never settled fully together. He was attentive enough after he took me to Saint Mary for the rest of my pregnancy and when we lived with his mother, but I was never able to regain the excitement and expectations of those days when I turned sixteen— when he had taught me how to be a woman. I was never able to recapture the emotions and the overwhelming feeling of safety and security that he had instilled in me during those long drives into the country or from that first weekend we spent together. The first weekend we were together (when he drunk and played dominoes with his friends) he had not treated me as if my body was all that he wanted. I felt a love for him that night—a love I was never able to recapture after the death of my friend.

We tried various businesses together and finally made a success of furniture manufacturing and selling. That part of our lives turned out well.

My parents leased their shop, and spent their days pottering in the fields. Like the old people around them, they remained strong and well.

I saw Madge at social events a few times over the years: in Kingston and Montego Bay. She retained her radiance. No one would ever have suspected that Robert and I had taken her only child from her. Madge and I never spoke, although it was clear we saw each other. She lived with someone I heard, but she never got married or had any more children.

I travelled and discovered Europe and North America. Once after I had been abroad for a month, one of the housekeepers welcomed me by saying, "It is good to have the real Mrs. Dove back."

Months later, Robert told me that one of the women who worked as a cashier at our local supermarket was pregnant with his child. Only then did I find out that during the past year while I was visiting my parents and travelling abroad, the young girl who was pregnant with his child had moved into our home with her mother, and the young girl and Robert had stayed in our bedroom.

During a sardonic row, he told me he wanted me to leave our home so the expecting mother of his unborn child could move in.

"Why?" I asked. "After all we have been through together."

"Why?" he repeated, as if I were a fool. "You of all people should understand."

4 TWO SISTERS' CHILDREN

There is no perfection, only life.
~ Milan Kundera ~

Daisy was visiting her daughter Rebecca and granddaughter Anna in Hanover. Rebecca and her daughter Anna had both recently arrived from England for the holidays.

Spending Christmas and heralding in the New Year in Jamaica was a tradition that went back many years for Rebecca and Anna. This year was particularly important because Rebecca was turning sixty, Anna was turning thirty, and Rebecca would start living part-time in both England and Jamaica. Rebecca and Anna were in the throes of planning a birthday-housewarming party.

Over the past week, Daisy felt like she had been watching a reel of film fast-forwarding through sixty years—unbelievable. Since her arrival from her home in Kingston, Daisy found herself repeatedly saying the number of years aloud, "*Sixty* years." Although it didn't feel like it to her, there were really more years than sixty. There was the time before she and Fitz were married—the years before Rebecca was born.

Daisy cried the whole day after she gave birth to Rebecca, fearful that she would not be alive to see Rebecca go to nursery school. There were tears after the other three children too, but those tears were for herself.

There were grandchildren and great-grandchildren now, and Daisy was grateful she was still alive to see them. She saw them at least once a year on the anniversary of her husband's death, and Daisy always returned to England for that anniversary. Sometimes, if she was lucky, she saw them more often: when one or her children surprised her with a ticket to go back to England for her birthday, for one of her children's birthdays, or to witness the birth a great-grandchild.

Daisy's youngest daughter, Kay, periodically tried to persuade Daisy to return to England to live. Now that their father was dead, she argued there was no reason for her to remain in Jamaica. But Daisy had no intention of leaving Jamaica again to live in England.

Daisy told her daughter that she was very comfortable and content in Jamaica. She told herself that being in Jamaica and free at last from the burden of her marriage was like walking home with heavy steps then suddenly remembering that the home once suffused with pain and disappointment had been demolished and replaced with a new one—a light and joyous one.

Five years earlier when Rebecca's father died, the family came to Jamaica for his funeral. Rebecca, stricken with grief and lamenting that her beloved father would be in the cold earth in Jamaica and her mother all alone, decided she would buy land in Jamaica. Shortly thereafter while she and Anna were on their way from Kingston to spend a weekend in Negril, they saw a sign advertising land for sale in Hanover.

Less than a year later, Rebecca and Anna, who did almost everything together, bought a one-acre plot and started building their house. It took them almost two years to complete the house, but it was now their pride and joy. Rebecca was looking forward to the party, but she looked forward to showing off the house to her guests even more.

Starting this year, Rebecca planned to live between the two

countries: six months in Jamaica, six months in England. She planned to relocate fully to Jamaica within five years.

Rebecca had been long since divorced. Her marriage lasted just long enough for her to have the child she greatly desired. Soon after the birth of her only child, Anna, Rebecca dispensed with the husband that, if truth be told, she had not wanted in the first place. She had bowed to her mother's pressure to marry when she had got pregnant with Anna.

"You can't do that to the baby," her mother had insisted. But to Rebecca, her mother's insistence seemed without conviction.

Rebecca's father had disagreed with Daisy. "Marriage doesn't matter anymore. You either love someone, or you don't. And if you do, marriage is the least of it," he had said. "And of course, more children are born out of wedlock than you would believe."

Rebecca's decision to relocate to Jamaica, albeit for only six months at first, was a dream come true for Daisy. Daisy could never admit it to her other children, but Rebecca held a special place in her heart. Rebecca was the only one of her four children who had been born in Jamaica—when Fitz had been all hers. If only she had stopped there. Rebecca would have been her Anna—her one and only, her everything.

Daisy considered Rebecca and Anna's affection for one another unconventional, but she admired their relationship. Except for the years Anna spent at university and doing her medical training, Rebecca and Anna never lived apart. They even travelled together and invested together. They jointly owned a successful medical practice in Surrey in southeast England and lived together in an expansive property in the same county.

Rebecca was Daisy's favourite child, and Anna her favourite grandchild. Anna was a lot like Rebecca, Daisy always thought, only more certain than her mother. Daisy did not always understand or agree with her granddaughter's views, but she liked the way Anna defined herself without needing to reference ages-old beliefs and traditions. Anna planned to have children alone, as she repeatedly told her grandmother. When the time was right, she would sell her medical practice and join her mother in Jamaica. Marriage had never been a part of Anna's ambitions. "Marriage is an utter joke," was her refrain.

Three days before the party while the three women were having breakfast, Rebecca told a story about a friend who was going through a particularly bitter divorce—one that finally came after years of loveless coexistence. "And there wasn't even sex to compensate," Rebecca reported. "My friend told me that her husband stopped being of any use a long time ago."

"I cannot see why any rational person would be surprised about that," Anna said, not disguising her impatience. "It goes against human nature and rationality. Having sex with the same person for thirty years must be frightful."

"That's ambitious, my dear. Few men can be of any use for that length of time," her mother said, with a grin.

"Some of us grew up thinking we had to stay. Good sex, bad sex, or no sex that was the least of it," Daisy rang in. "In my day, many of us only wanted to have our children in the proper way. And hoped there would be companionship in our old age."

Anna laughed. "The proper way? Grandma, please. People might as well not bother if our family is anything to go by. Marriage is an utter joke," she continued, repeating her refrain.

Those words were like a knife to Daisy's heart. Failed marriages or the pretence of marriage had become the norm in their family. Three of her children were divorced and her grandchild was now swearing she did not believe in marriage. In Daisy's time, growing up in Saint Catherine, getting married was a triumph. Daisy sat silently with her thoughts. *Did Louisa and Fitz put a curse on the family?*

On the day before the party while visiting Fort Charlotte and Hanover Parish Church in Lucea, an almond tree in the church yard caught Daisy's attention and reminded her of her youth. Among the tree's plentiful, green, shiny leaves was a solitary, golden leaf shivering in the light breeze with the others. The golden leaf reminded her of herself all those years ago when she was the only young woman in her district married at the tender age of nineteen. Daisy had even married before her older sister Louisa, and Louisa was four years her senior. Daisy basked in the respect and admiration she received for being married before her older sister. Daisy had boasted that she was untouched before her wedding night: a boast that resurfaced with recurrent regret over the years. As she walked along, she couldn't help but wonder: *Does anyone consider that a virtue anymore? Or is it just a cause for astonishment? What is it like to experience more than one man in a lifetime? Different caresses. Different kisses. Different everything.* How she wished she had experienced other men.

Rebecca and Anna's house was in a small town outside the coastal town of Lucea. Their house was a stone's throw from the Caribbean Sea and set on a cliff with a sheer drop to the beach. To get to the natural white-sand beach from their house, you had to walk past one of two neighbouring gated developments, follow down a path, and then navigate some steep steps. The beach, less than two hundred metres long, was precious to Rebecca and Anna. They called it their private beach and hardly walked on it without reflecting on how blessed and lucky they felt to live so close to it. Few people knew the beach was there, and many of those who did were too spoilt by the easy access of Negril's pristine, seven-mile, white-sand beach a few miles up the road that they couldn't be bothered with the uneven, often slippery, stone steps.

Before the new highway was built, their town had been on the main road to Negril, the most western town on the island. Now even though there was a sign pointing to their little town and to the newer gated developments that sandwiched their little town, only people who lived or had business there chanced through.

So far, none of the houses where Rebecca and Anna lived needed burglar bars, high-fenced walls, ferocious guard dogs, or armed guards at the touch of a panic button to be safe and secure. Instead, there were small, white-picket fences and wooden gates with old-fashion, metal catches. Cascading above and over the fences and gates were bougainvillea of all colours, delicate pink hibiscus, and an occasional poinciana tree. Along the four or so roads that made up the town, occasionally there were fruit trees (mangoes, coconuts, June plums, and avocado pears), as if planted for the public good. There were dogs in the area too—miniature ones with ferocious barks belying their size but in character with their oversized self-esteems.

The mornings were typically bright and sunny. The sun, the natural clock, got them up at six o'clock for their morning walk. Daisy loved their morning walks together.

Every morning, including this morning, the three of them walked to the beach, swam, and played with the dogs. Every day one of them commented about the benefits of natural vitamin D. Typical of that time of day, the sun suddenly got too hot, so they heeded their cue and sauntered back to eat breakfast.

After the walk, Daisy went to rest on Rebecca's wraparound veranda, Rebecca prepared breakfast with the housekeeper and Anna made phone calls to her office in England.

While resting peacefully on the veranda, Daisy absentmindedly watched an ocean liner and sailboats bob and float in the cool crisp sea. On its way to perhaps Mobay, Falmouth, or Ocho Rios, the ocean liner dwarfed the sailboats. The thought of people having fun on a cruise ship made Daisy wistful. She was regretful that so much of her life had been spent joyless.

The weather threatened to be overcast in the afternoon, as it had been every day for the past week. Over the past week, there had been dramatic thunderstorms in the afternoons. The unpropitious claps sent Brownie (their shih tzu Pekingese) into a frenzied panic, seeking safety among a cluttered clothes closet or an equivalent enclosed area. Just when he thought he was safe, an even louder thunder would come, chasing him into another room. They often took turns embracing his shivering body, but they couldn't hold him for the entire afternoon.

Oblivious to Brownie, the thunderstorms brought large heavy raindrops, which made discordant (yet comforting) music on the roof. The storms also rapidly transformed the sea from translucent turquoise to cloudy grey.

"I hope it won't be like this for the party tomorrow," Anna said, as she finished her telephone conversation and joined her grandmother on the veranda.

"It won't matter. We have enough covered area to keep everyone dry but still outside," Daisy replied.

"I am worried about people not coming if the rain catches them at home. You know Jamaicans are frightened of rain. I've ordered so much food."

"Do you want a drink, Grandma?" Anna asked, with the *ma* full and extended.

"No, thank you, my darling, I have some water here on the floor beside me."

Including her perfectly enunciated English, everything about Anna fascinated her grandmother. Daisy often smiled to herself when they were out together. Everyone seemed to notice Anna, following her with their eyes from her wonderfully proportioned facial features to her thick, well-kept locks and her tiny, well-exercised frame. Some people rested their eyes momentarily and others rested them longer on her pert backside before their eyes continued down her slender, seemingly-never-ending legs. A few undaunted called out, "Empress!" It was a wonder to Daisy how Anna didn't seem to notice any of it, and if she did, was uncaring of the attention. None of the attention made her giddy as similar attention had made Daisy when she was young.

Daisy had met a few of the men who had hankered after her granddaughter. Daisy wavered between feeling sorry for Anna's admirers and laughing at them. Anna was never going to be shackled.

Anna had her e-reader in her hand but had not turned it on yet. Daisy had a book open, but turned facedown, on her lap. Passion for reading ran through Daisy's side of the family, and it crossed several generations.

Anna wanted to broach a topic with her grandmother that she knew would cause her grandmother upset. Nonetheless, Anna felt compelled, but anxious, to speak to her grandmother sooner rather than later. Daisy was eighty years old, and in the past few months, Daisy's health had deteriorated. Anna realized that Daisy would not be with them forever, and she wanted to hear Daisy tell her side of the story.

Two years earlier at the third anniversary of Fitz's death, Anna heard whispered talk that fired her interest. As usual for the event, Daisy was in England visiting family. Over the years, one or another of Daisy's children had asked why their mother preferred to be in England at that time and not in Jamaica where Fitz had died and was buried. Daisy had never explained and her children did not press the point, it was not a secret that their parents had not enjoyed a happy marriage.

A few days after the third anniversary of her father's death, Rebecca received a message that her cousin William, who had migrated to Canada from England some years earlier, had recently taken ill with a stroke. A few months later another stroke took his life.

William was one of two children of Anna's late Great-Aunt Louisa. Their families had always been close, and William's death was hard on the family. William's death was especially hard on Rebecca for several reasons: they were both born in Jamaica, they were both born in the same house that the two sisters shared with their husbands, and she was only a few months older than him.

As an adult, Anna thought she understood their complete family history. Daisy was the first of the two sisters to migrate to England. Louisa, her husband Jake, and their young son William joined Daisy, Fitz, and their young daughter in England a couple of years later. Fitz and Daisy had already bought a large house, and the two families lived together until Louisa and Jake purchased their own house on the adjacent road. For the children, separate houses and the road apart made little difference. The two homes were as one with their Aunt Louisa's the most trampled.

On the day they received news about William's illness, Kay was visiting Rebecca and they were talking in the living room. The door to the living room was ajar, and as she was passing by the door, Anna overheard Kay speaking: "The oddest thing happened the other day. I connected with someone on Facebook recently who I knew at school. Her name is Janice. Do you remember her?"

Rebecca shook her head no.

"Janice and I met for coffee a few times, and recently we had dinner together. Janice and William were at secondary school together. Janice said William told her years ago that he and I share the same father. I laughed at her of course. Can you imagine her saying something like that? How could people make up such lies? For what reason?"

Feeling like she was hearing something not meant for her ears, Anna called out, "I'm off. Back later."

Anna did not like her aunt Kay. When Kay visited without her daughters or husband, Dave, Anna invariably excused herself and went to another part of the house or left the house. It irritated Anna that no one else in the family saw Kay as the manipulative, pathetic, and persona non grata that Anna thought she was.

"I know we are in debt," Anna once overheard Kay tell Rebecca, "but I don't want to know the ins and outs. Dave is responsible for all the bills."

Kay took and left jobs at will, as if her monetary contributions to her family were inconsequential. Rebecca often lent her sister money, knowing it would never be returned. Anna often quarrelled with Rebecca about the money she had lent Kay over the years, but now Anna left the topic alone. For the most part, Kay continued to infuriate Anna, and Anna only occasionally tolerated her aunt for her mom's sake. Anna suspected that Rebecca merely tolerated her sister because doing so made her light shine a little brighter. Anna did not believe her mother could love or respect a woman who did not make her mark on life—sister or no sister.

Later that evening after Kay left, Anna asked Rebecca, "Is it true? Did Granddaddy father William with my Great-Aunt Louisa? Weren't your parents supposed to have had a perfect marriage? Well, according to Grandma they did."

Rebecca sighed. The conversation with Kay still weighed heavily on her mind. Rebecca did not have the energy to go over the story again at least not immediately. "Where did you get that from? I don't know that Mummy has ever said that, Anna. They didn't separate, if that's how Mummy defined perfect."

"That's not fair. They must have been happy. They seemed close to me, anyway. Plus, they were together for well over fifty years. Not many people stay married for that long these days."

Rebecca sniggered. "I suppose for Mummy that was success. There were never real dramatics in the house. Mummy and Daddy just got on with things." Rebecca hesitated. "Even if there was little love between them."

"You have never told me you thought that."

"It has never come up."

"What did Granddaddy tell you? You and he were close," Anna said.

"I was close to Mummy too. I am close to Mummy."

"I know, but you and Granddaddy were always talking," Anna

insisted.

"How do you know whether or not we were close? You weren't paying attention to us. When you were old enough, you had your head in your books. Then you went away at college."

"Who said I wasn't aware? Besides, I adored him, and everyone knows I was his favourite grandchild."

Rebecca shook her head. "You are a joker. Daddy never told you that."

"Yes, he did. Well, he said I was his favourite, but he also said he told that to all the other grandchildren too." Anna laughed.

Rebecca became serious and contemplated telling Anna what Fitz had told her four years earlier. Now that Rebecca had told Kay, it was only a matter of time before everyone in the family knew, and she did not want Anna to hear it from anyone else.

There were so many reasons why Rebecca had not found the words to tell Anna: shame, anger, not wanting Anna to remember Fitz or Louisa in a poor light.

"Mum, you haven't answered my question though. Is it true? Was Granddaddy William's and Jacintha's father? How could that be?"

Rebecca groaned, "He was."

"What?"

"Yes, Daddy told me everything just after Aunt Louisa died. He and Aunt Louisa lived a double life for years. They were lovers while they lived in Jamaica, before they migrated to England."

"No way!" Anna exclaimed. "No way," she repeated.

"Yes," Rebecca said heavily. In one sense Rebecca was relieved that she had finally unburden to Anna.

~~~~~

Louisa's breast cancer had taken her within months of her diagnosis, leaving both sides of the family in shock and disbelief. Daisy accepted her sister's death with seemingly calculated coldness.

"There has to be some punishment for evil," Daisy had said to Rebecca when Louisa died. Daisy refused to elucidate when an upset and grieving Rebecca challenged her mother about the comment.

There were no sisterly tears from Daisy, no sentimental speeches at the memorial service in London. Louisa had asked to be buried in Jamaica, and she was. Daisy refused to attend the funeral, so Rebecca went with her father, her aunt's husband, and her cousins, William and Jacintha.

Not long after the funeral and her return from Jamaica, Rebecca spoke to her father. "This might not be the right time, Daddy, but Mummy called Aunt Louisa evil. Why? What happened between them? I know they were always squabbling. But evil?"

Fitz and Rebecca were together at the dining table having tea and digestive biscuits. He took such a long time to answer that Rebecca thought he wasn't going to reply.

"The fault is all mine," her father said finally.

Rebecca waited, watching steadily as her father sipped the piping hot tea.

"They are my children: William and Jacintha. Both of them belong to me," he said slowly.

Rebecca's body slumped then became rigid as if she were a puppet. For moments, she did not move.

"I knew Louisa first, you know, knew and loved her even before I knew your mother."

"Why did you marry Mummy then?" Rebecca's words were almost inaudible.

Fitz had a hand over his mouth, as if trying to stifle his words. "It wasn't intentional. Louisa and Daisy's parents were very strict, especially their father. He protected his daughters. There were stories that he had a boy sent to jail overnight on some made-up charge, just because the boy called on one of his daughters."

"Louisa and I use to meet in secret, though." Fitz looked fully at his daughter. His face was now relaxed, almost smiling. "She even got pregnant once," then quietly, he added, "but lost the baby before she started to show. I was with her when the bleeding and clotting happened. Lord, we were frightened. We were both only nineteen. After that, she got scared and didn't want me to come near her. I think she blamed me because I begged her to see the woman who 'fixed' such things. She said I put a hex on our baby."

Fitz drifted into reverie again. Rebecca lost her appetite for tea and biscuits.

Fitz continued, "I was nineteen and poor, and I was afraid of her powerful father. To be honest, I did pray with all my heart for Louisa to lose the baby. I pleaded with her to try and stop it. But I am not God. I didn't cause her to lose the baby. And after she lost the baby, she stopped speaking to me completely. I tried to find ways to see her. I eventually got a job on her father's property. I did everything I could to please her father, and I did please him in the end. Her father saw that I was a good worker and that I was willing to do what he wanted me to do. I think he grew to like me as the son he did not have."

"For years, I tried to win Louisa back, but she wouldn't give me the time of day. I foolishly started paying attention to your mother, thinking it would make Louisa jealous and make her come back to me. My stupid actions only made things worse. When she took up with Jake, I knew I had lost."

"The day I married your mother, Louisa told me that I was going to give her back the child I took from her. I am not blaming Louisa, mind you. I loved her then, and I loved her to the day she died. I was married to your mother. I cared for your mother, but it was Louisa that I have always loved and wanted. She was my true wife."

Rebecca and her father sat in silence for a considerable period of time. Rebecca could find no words. Fitz had found the words to speak aloud what had been silent in him for years.

"I don't know how I'm going to live without her. In fact, I don't know if I want to live now that she is gone," he said finally.

Rebecca had carefully listened to her father tell his story of betrayal. Now, she was not thinking about him or about her mother. She was thinking about her cousins, her half siblings, William and

Jacintha.

Questions began racing through her head: *When were William and Jacintha told? Had they been told? By whom? Had Fitz loved, albeit secretly, and treasured them as he had Rebecca and her siblings?*

Rebecca felt a deep and indescribable sadness for her newly discovered siblings, especially for William who had died while the lies were still being told and the secret still buried.

"How did Mummy endure it? Why didn't you just separate?" Rebecca challenged her father.

"It was like a beam before us, but we never once spoke directly about it. Once or twice over the years, I suggested to your mother that we should separate and live honest lives. Daisy would not have it, nor would Louisa for that matter. Daisy was frightened of what it would do to all of you—all the children."

"The children came into it then, did we?" Rebecca sneered. "Unbelievable. And how about her husband? How about Jake? Did he know? How could he not have known?"

"He knew. Of course, he knew. How could he, in truth, not know? He was her husband. But Jake and Louisa had an understanding. They were husband and wife in public, but they lived like brother and sister in private. Yet, Jake loved her too. How could anyone not love a woman like Louisa?"

~~~~~

"Bloody hell! That is some mixed up crap. Is that why Jacintha disappeared from radar? Why she doesn't want anything to do with the family?" Anna said, then gasped.

Rebecca sighed heavily. "I imagine so. The strange thing is… I loved Aunt Louisa. I loved her too. We all loved her. You know how loveable she was because you, my siblings, and your cousins were all close to her," Rebecca said.

"I admired her a lot. I thought of her as a renaissance woman," Anna said. "I really admired and respected her."

Rebecca recalled that when she and her siblings were young and the sisters were sharing a house, the children from both sides of the family were often found in Louisa's part of the house. Later when Louisa and Jake had their own house, the children tended to congregate there.

"Remember how Aunt Louisa was always involved in one course or another at night school: baking, sewing, knitting, crocheting, cake decorating, flower arranging. Remember how she practiced on us.

God knows how we all kept slim after all the cakes and pies we ate. And she made money from them too. Sewing and baking for weddings and events. She made a lot of money from her skills."

"Perhaps the night school thing was a rouse," Anna countered.

Rebecca and Anna laughed together, easing Rebecca's discomfort. It was not easy for Rebecca to air her parents' dirty laundry and express her profound love for a woman who had flouted conventions and caused her mother so much hurt.

Rebecca told Anna that when they were growing up Daisy would often find reasons to quarrel with Louisa about where the children chose to spend most of their time when they were not in school. Rebecca told Anna that Daisy had often accused Aunt Louisa of having no rules so that the children preferred to spend more time at her home.

Rebecca said, "When I was a teenager, I remember periods when inexplicable misery overcame my mother. Sometimes it seemed like she spent months under an impenetrable cloud that no one in the family could lift. Those times for me were unbearable, and I found excuses to avoid her and spend most of my time at Aunt Louisa's house."

"That must have made it even worse for Grandma," Anna said, feeling sad. "You were leaving Grandma to be with the very person who was causing her hurt."

"I imagine so," Rebecca said. "Sometimes I feel sad about that, other times I feel angry. Mum colluded, the four of them did—Mum, Dad, Aunt Louisa, and Uncle Jake. They chose that life."

Anna agreed with Rebecca but said that she understood the pain that the sisters and their husbands must have endured.

"Why did Granddaddy and Grandma move to Jamaica so soon after Aunt Louisa died then? It's odd that they both went together."

Rebecca felt compelled to explain what had happened.

"You were away at medical school, so you didn't notice that after Louisa's funeral my dad changed. He hardly spoke and sat most of the day staring at whatever was on TV. He became more like himself after he decided he had to permanently return to Jamaica. He insisted that he would return alone even if Mum did not want to go." Rebecca sighed, remembering both the sadness that clouded her father in that period following Louisa's death and the resigned pain of Daisy.

"Mum, of course, went with him. And it was less than a year after they landed in Jamaica that Dad died."

~~~~~

It was now two years since Rebecca's revelation to Anna about Fitz and Louisa. Anna had seen Daisy at least once each year since then and had wanted to talk to her about it. Rebecca had always dissuaded her, stating that Daisy would get upset and be outraged.

Anna was not convinced but had decided to bide her time. But, with the party just hours away and Daisy joyous about Rebecca slowly relocating to Jamaica, Anna thought the time was right to hear Daisy's side. Wrenching questions raced through Anna's conscious: *How did Daisy tolerate what Fitz did? Why did she stay married to him?*

"Grandmummy," Anna started, with a term of endearment she used when she was in a particularly loving mood. Her grandfather had always been Granddaddy, but the extra term of endearment was used sparingly for her grandmother. "Is it true that Granddaddy was William's and Jacinta's father?"

Anna had not bargained for the look that came over Daisy. Her face shrouded in a confusion of shocked disbelief, sadness, and outrage. It was moments until Daisy collected herself and spoke.

"Anna, for as long as I live, I ask you not to raise that

conversation with me. Never raise that idle conversation with me again."

Anna, stunned at her grandmother's vehemence, felt she should apologise, but she knew that attempting to do so would be insincere. She was not sorry; she was angry that her grandmother was still refusing to face the truth of her life.

Daisy got up from the dining table and left Anna alone. She went to her room and sat heavily on the bed. Suddenly exhausted, she laid down. Memories of the years with Fitz and her knowledge that most of their life together had been for show came flooding back. She felt ashamed and sad. Shame and sadness had long replaced the anger that she lived with for over half a century when he was alive and loving Louisa.

Daisy fell asleep for a short time and dreamt. In the dream she saw Louisa and Fitz standing by the bank of a river. The swollen river flowed with the clearest water Daisy could ever imagine. Fitz and Louisa were looking in Daisy's direction but they did not see her. They seemed to be looking intently at something else. Daisy looked around to see what the pair of them were looking at but found nothing extraordinary. When she returned her gaze to where they had been, Fitz and Louisa were gone.

Daisy woke to the sound of new voices: decorators had come and food preparation was underway. Anna does not deserve my anger, Daisy thought. There and then Daisy decided she would have to a find way to talk to her granddaughter before Anna returned to England. She would explain everything to her: what happened, how she felt, why she stayed with Fitz, and how she had loved him to the end. Daisy did not want to leave Anna with the belief that she had lived and died in a morass of anger and bitterness. It was too late to convince Rebecca, but it was not too late for Anna. Maybe there were too many layers of conflicting emotions for Rebecca to negotiate, but hopefully she could make Anna understand.

It was never lost on Daisy how Rebecca loved and admired her Aunt Louisa and Fitz as much or even more than how Rebecca loved her. It used to wound and hurt Daisy that Rebecca's love for her was not sacrosanct. Daisy had worked on that hurt over the years and had slowly come to terms with it. But sometimes Daisy reflected, *At least I can still enjoy Rebecca's love—Louisa and Fitz cannot.*

About a year or so after Fitz died, Rebecca had tried to raise the subject of Louisa and Fitz with Daisy. But Daisy had quickly given

Rebecca short shrift. No one else had ever raised the topic with Daisy: not her other children, not friends, not associates. Daisy was aware of the rumours that had gone on over the years, but she handled them the same way she handled her life—in her own way. What had always amazed Daisy was that the children had not cottoned on to what had gone on between their parents over the years.

After napping, Daisy left her room just before lunchtime. She took her favourite seat by the pool and watched with quiet joy as the house was transformed for the party. The florist brought huge arrangements of fresh flowers and was placing them on tables and wooden pedestals around the pool and on tables in the sitting room. Single-stem orchids hung on the poolside gazebo with invisible threads keeping them in place and adding even more magic.

The event organizer unfolded several circular, eight-seater tables and spread a gleamingly white tablecloth on each table. Young people dressed in black-and white attire arrived together and set each table with delicate red wine and white wine glasses, water goblets, gold charger plates, fine-china dinner plates, and antique silverware. The most eye-catching feature, Daisy thought, was the long-trumpet vase placed in the centre of each table with arrangements of red tropical flowers delicately balanced on top.

The musician arrived and played some old-time reggae to test his sound system. Rebecca's joy and Anna's enthusiasm were contagious. Daisy watched them as they spoke with the planner and the planner's staff: praising, suggesting, and confirming each detail.

As Daisy watched the comings and goings, she whispered, "So strong and mighty, Louisa, where are you now? I am still here. Try as you did, you and Fitz did not destroy me." Daisy heard herself speak above the excitement of the party planning; she was relaxed and content. The dark impenetrable clouds—that had plagued her in the days when Fitz and Louisa controlled her life and her mind—no longer loomed.

The birthday party was a resounding success. The rain held off, and everyone who was invited appeared. The plentiful food, music, night sea breeze, and good company kept everyone until dawn.

Anna was surprised and delighted that her grandmother stayed up too, eating and occasionally moving a leg, as Daisy put it. Anna waltzed with her grandmother a few times—kissing and hugging her often throughout the evening.

5 THE WOMAN WITH A MOLE ON HER FACE

We are never deceived, we deceive ourselves.
~ Johann Wolfgang Goethe ~

She had a mole on the left side of her face just above her mouth. We were seated next to each other on the five a.m., luxury express bus going from Montego Bay to Kingston. There would be only one stop in Ocho Rios. The bus was due to arrive at nine a.m.; we would be neighbours for a short while.

She had the seat next to the window, facing the sea. Being January, it was still dark; the day was poised to unfold as we made our way along the North Coast.

For some reason, my eyes were drawn to the silhouette of her face—her strong, no-nonsense profile with perfect proportions. When she glanced my way only her large, light-brown eyes suggested vulnerability. Her striking eyes had long curly lashes and pupils that accentuated the whites. I caught a glimpse of them as she turned to gaze momentarily at the strapping man who had just slid into a seat in the opposite row. He caught my eye too, leaving me with a smile. But it was my immediate neighbour who compelled my attention.

I had noticed eyes like hers only a few times in my life; her eyes were distant, occasional, and protracted with a fixed stare. Her mouth curled downwards like a child's drawing of a sad face. Her skin may once have been nice, but now her skin looked tired and lifeless— carefully washed but only worthy of a dab of nondescript moisturizer.

At least once a month, I had business in Kingston, and I was tired of driving there and back in one day. I was invariably unable to sleep the night before, and I was petrified of falling asleep over the wheel, especially on the return journey. The strong coffee I was forced to drink kept me awake not only on my return journey but also throughout the night, making me doubly tired for days afterwards. The express bus was a welcomed option. By taking the bus, I avoided the intense concentration required behind the wheel and the madness of driving on the island. I had time to read, think, and people watch.

Traveling towards the slowly rising sun, the bus made its way from the bus park via Top Road, through the airport roundabout, past Flankers (the coconut man with his makeshift stall was not there yet), and then past the Blue Diamond Shopping Centre and further on the Rose Hall Great House while heading out of town on the main highway.

"I will never get used to the beauty at this time of year," the woman with the mole opened.

Her accent surprised me. It was the accent of an educated Kingstonian: perfect diction with that singsong intonation that felt like the comfort of home.

"Me neither," I replied, as I turned to meet her gaze. "It's amazing. Do you do this journey often?"

"Occasionally. I don't drive at night anymore, so I don't risk driving to Kingston just in case night catches me. My eyes can't take the car beams now. And none of me can take the bad driving. I used to think driving was bad only in town, but bad driving is all over the island now. Bad driving kills so many people."

I agreed with her.

"No courtesies these days," she ended, drifting back to her

thoughts.

I fished out my e-reader and found the novel I was reading. I was not one for befriending fellow travellers. It often irritated me when they wanted to talk. I tried, as best I could, to hold a leave-me-in-peace expression on my face. Some got the message, others didn't. The I'll-talk-to-you-whether-you-like-it-or-not travellers did just that, sometimes as if I was not there. Occasionally, these types interested me; but even when they did not interest me, I still practiced politeness. Courtesy prevented me from being rude and pointedly ignoring them.

I opened my e-reader to *Nervous Conditions* by Tsitsi Dangarembga and happily settled back into the company of the characters who had become my companions over the past week. It was my second reading of the book. I had read it when I was at university but wanted to read it again. When I started O-Level English Language all those years ago, I had been horrified when the teacher said we had to read each book on the list several times. I had been an avid reader for as long as I could remember, but reading a novel again…. Fortunately, Thomas Hardy's *Far from the Madding Crowd* and Emily Brontë's *Wuthering Heights* had wonderfully changed my mind. On the second, third, and even fourth reading of these novels, I discovered nuances and meanings that had escaped me on prior readings. Now, while in my fifties, straddling retirement, and helping my son with his business, I sought out books that had made an impression on me in years past and re-read them alongside new literary discoveries.

There were early morning bathers, just past the gas station in the town of Greenwood. It always pleased me to see them: men, women, and children taking early morning dips by the makeshift beach (the area lit only by vehicle lights with the bathers' torches carefully balanced on the rocks). There was no real beach, no sand, just a pile of naturally piled rocks leading into the sea.

"Some people would give their right arm to be so free," my neighbour offered.

I smiled but did not respond. I was not sure whether she was speaking to me or to herself. I waited for her to speak again, thinking I would respond then. The bus trundled on, leaving the bathers to enjoy the cool Caribbean Sea.

The sun, a hazy yellow glow, was rising and peeling away the dawn. The relatively long stretch of road from Falmouth to Ocho Rios was quiet. Only the occasional red-plated minibus sped through the dawn, heading towards Falmouth or Montego Bay, where we had come from. The cars, buses, and trucks going in our direction easily overtook the bus and disappeared in the distance as the bus held steady to the legal speed of eighty kilometres an hour.

As the bus approached Discovery Bay, I overheard the strapping neighbour discuss a recent gun murder in Saint James.

"They say we have more churches per square mile in this country than in any other country. Every minute you hear one or another of them is having a revival, convention, or prayer breakfast. They are clearly not making any impact on the gunmen."

"Something is not right, somewhere," his neighbour said.

I dozed off and woke to the sound of my neighbour's voice. I was not sure if she was talking to me or to herself, but I responded.

"Sorry? I drifted off." I said. "So lovely to be driven."

"Yes, always nice," she said. "I am going to see my husband."

"I see. Is he working in Kingston?"

"Oh, no, not anymore. He's dead."

"Oh, gosh, I'm sorry. So sorry."

"No need to be sorry," she said slowly. Then added, as if pondering, "I'm glad it's over."

Thoughts about her caring for a long-time sick husband and her relief that he was now out of his suffering came to my mind. That would explain the eyes, I thought. I felt sorry for judging her, for framing her in a story I could never know.

"No need to be sorry," she repeated. "He turned into a complete dog. If I had had the strength, I would have killed him myself years ago. I actually tried to hire a gunman once," she announced. "But I lost my nerve at the last minute."

I had not planned the startled "Oh."

She continued to speak—as if to herself—as if my listening was incidental to her telling.

The start of her story was not unlike other stories often told around the island: man marries, man serially cheats on wife, man has children outside the marriage, wife stays with husband, wife assumes role of the long-suffering, bitter martyr.

~~~~~

"I know none of that is unique to me," she said. "My story is that I could not get beyond it. I know everyone thought I did. I was the kept woman who lived a charmed life by all appearances. But I always wanted to work. My husband viewed his wife working outside the house as a personal insult to him. His wife could never work. So I took care of the big, beautiful house he provided for us from his big successful business, and I bore and cared for our three beautiful children until they got their big jobs just like he had done. But all the while, there was another me: angry, plotting. What a terrible way to have wasted my life."

~~~~~

As we were passing Puerto Seco Beach (almost hidden now behind high-walled fences), vague memories of Sunday School trips from Saint Catherine to this beach struggled to take form. The name rather than any actual day on the beach took shape.

Perhaps she has never unburdened to anyone, I thought, as she continued her story.

~~~~~

"We were only twenty-one and just out of university when we married. Not our fault really. I suppose we both had our reasons. My reasons were the good family he came from and the business he would get from his father. I had no doubt he would give me a good life, nor did our families who had been friends for years. Of course, I can never be sure why he chose me. He had lots of girls who would have said yes. My looks? My family name? We all know that looks always turn out to be the least of it. Family name?"

~~~~~

The woman sniggered but did not give her assessment. Family name was a big issue on the island. *What is the experience of those inside that world?* I imagined that having or acquiring an honourable or famous family name was much like having other prized and envied qualities—like beauty, education, success, or fame. Possessors of these prized qualities still had to live and manoeuver their way through life's challenges. I suspected that people who attained these prized possessions navigated through life with only slightly more ease than the unattractive, uneducated, unsuccessful, or unknown.

~~~~~

"Women loved my husband, and it was not difficult to understand why. But for some reason, he hardly got along with men. He always seemed to be knocking heads with men. There were some dramatic fallings out over the years and always with rumours that a woman was involved. I tried not to listen to the rumours. I would have gone mad long ago if I had."

"He had a lot of enemies in the end. Not enemies in the sense that they would have harmed him, but enemies nonetheless. Some of his enemies were men we knew well, men who moved in our circle but did not tolerate him in their homes. I lost a lot of friends because of him. I was quite isolated in some ways. I only had the children and my sisters after he died—that's why I left Kingston."

"It was always interesting watching him socialize with other men, especially at business or association meetings. I couldn't understand why so many men had fallings-out with him. Even some who were once his good friend: like Jerry. My husband and his enemies all went to the same school and the same university. They even played club cricket together."

"I suppose that is why he went into business with an older woman. Jane was unmarried and no-nonsense, and she gave everything to the business. She was not distracted by him, and he was not distracted by her."

~~~~~

The midnight blue that had covered the sea was slowly giving way to a light blue in the distance trimmed with turquoise at the edges. The mountains to the south were taking on a bluey-green hue. In an hour or so, almost every sapling would be visible from a distance.

The sky would be limpid blue. There would be no rain today.

I got off the bus at the rest stop in Ocho Rios. The bus had left Montego Bay with a few empty seats; now, new passengers filled the empty seats. There was a man in a stall selling snacks and hot tea. I bought a cup of peppermint tea and a banana. I ate the banana outside the bus, conscious that some passengers may not like the fruit's strong smell. My neighbour came off the bus too. I saw her go down the short passageway towards the restrooms. She was the last to re-enter the bus.

I was relieved the work to lay new water pipes was now finally done, so we could go through the Fern Gully rainforest to Kingston instead of having to go the Chalky Hill route. People insisted that going through Chalky Hill took minutes off the journey, but that route has never been preferred by me, even though some parts along Chalky Hill are visually stunning. The uneven and potholed road through Chalky Hill was too unpredictable. One month, the road might be perfect; another time (especially if there had been heavy rains) there would be one pothole after another. Trucks were not allowed through Fern Gully which was another bonus. And if you got stuck behind a truck along certain stretches of the Chalky Hill route, the journey could be exceptionally slow-going.

She started talking again as the bus entered the cool of Fern Gully and picked its way around the relay of bends and steadily climbed though the rain forest, passing dense ferns, and foliage that made up the rainforest and stalls that dotted the roadside, with vendors selling carvings and fabrics.

~~~~~

"He grew fat over the years. He was not an old man, but he looked like one. When our children were in their twenties and none of them no longer at home anymore, I tried to ward off the boredom that results when children are not around to occupy your time."

"In the early days of our marriage, I used to visit his office, sometimes meeting him for lunch, but it soon became uncomfortable for me. Embarrassingly, I saw it in the posture of the women at the office: gloating, ridicule, maybe even pity. I am no fool—not then, not now."

~~~~~

Suddenly, the brakes screeched then the passengers lurched forwards. The compulsory seat belts had done their job: we pitched forwards then safely backwards into our seats. A few passengers exclaimed. A speeding car had tried to overtake the bus and narrowly avoided collision with an oncoming minibus by swinging in sharply. Our bus would have careered into the rear of the speeding car, if not for the fast reaction of our driver.

My neighbour shook her head knowingly and then continued with her story.

~~~~~

"The doctors told him he needed to lose weight because he had hypertension, but he kept putting off the start date of his diet and often forgot to take his medication. I cooked healthy food, but he didn't always eat with me at home (except for some Saturdays and Sundays). He had better places to eat the other five days of the week."

"When they called me and said he had had a stroke at work, I wasn't surprised. The children were all living abroad by then; he wasn't quite fifty. I have to admit, I couldn't help the wry smile that crept on my face when I saw his twisted face and lifeless, limp body on a bed in the government hospital. The children came, thinking he was near death. Eventually, we moved him to a private hospital and then home. The children went back home to their lives and sent a specially designed bed for him. We moved him into one of the two guest bedrooms downstairs. The two guest bedrooms shared a common hall and bathroom. When the guest bedrooms' doors were open, activity in one room was visible in the other. Our bedroom and the children's bedrooms were upstairs."

"We had a live-in helper, of course, and nurses came to take care of him day and night. I moved my quarters downstairs to the guest room opposite his room, to be nearby. I watched the caregivers from my room as they moved around bathing, feeding, and taking care of him. I went into the room every day and stood for minutes looking at him."

"Soon the visits from his workers petered out along with visits from his business partner, Jane. Jane made me an offer to buy him out, which I accepted of course. His prognosis was not good, money was never an issue, the children were not interested in the responsibility, and what did I know about the business world?"

~~~~~

While making the steady climb over Mount Rosser, the bus passed uniformed schoolchildren waiting for their taxis. Some of the children seemed too young to be walking on their own along roads with no pavement and speeding vehicles.

I marvelled each time we passed a home or home-like structure perched on the hillside. Each structure was almost buried underneath the road, with the road as its rooftop and an unmistakeable black water tank barely visible beside it. Frequent water lockouts by the water commission made these tanks essential.

In Ewarton, we passed two policemen with their mandatory speed guns. One of the officers was bending over a car door and talking to a taxi driver.

"I wonder how much he has to give him?" said the strapping neighbour loudly. A few passengers groaned knowingly.

~~~~~

"The odd thing is that after he had the stroke, I began to feel happy for the first time in years. For one thing, I always knew where he was, and for another, I could see him whenever I wished. Only then did I realise that I had been holding a nagging worry for him. A worry that started when we were young, when he was well and going about behind my back leaving me home and alone. The worry I had for him had been eating away at me for twenty-eight years. It was only after I saw him helpless that the pent up rage, disappointment, and bitterness started to flow through and eventually out of me—like a long protracted sigh. A sigh that released itself without any action or attention from me."

"After he stabilised, he did not need the night nurse anymore. The day nurse still came and looked after him, saw to his medication, took this and that measurement, kept his chart, and fed and bathed him."

"The first man I brought home was Jerry. First, I took Jerry to see my husband; then, I had my husband watch us as we visited. My husband, helpless and unable to speak, laid there powerless. But I read my husband's eyes and watched his twisted mouth make sounds, as if to speak, but unable to form a single word. There was only a gargled sound from his throat: like someone needing to throw up but failing."

"Jerry was, of course, married, but that didn't concern me. I led him. I was the leader, and I was the leader with all the other lovers too. I seduced them—a skill I had long forgotten I had. The helper's quarters was in a cottage away from the house. The helper would have seen Jerry's car come and go, leaving late at night and occasionally in the early morning. But it was not the helper that concerned me; I wanted him to hear and see us together."

~~~~~

My neighbour smiled brightly, incongruous with the stillness and blank stare of her eyes.

~~~~~

"The scene still tickles me. Jerry, at my insistence, always went in to say hello to him before leaving with a wave and going into the adjoining guest room that I used to entertain my lovers. It tickles me even now to imagine his face as Jerry and I romped, laughed too loudly, and made love too noisily—as I exaggerated the climax of my enjoyment."

"He lasted nearly three years—going from a bed to a wheelchair on the veranda, to a spot under the mango tree in our garden. Occasionally, the nurse would take him to the beach and sit with him for the day. The children visited once or twice a year. The grandchildren spoke to him as if they were speaking to a baby who they thought could not hear and who they knew could not form words."

"There were a couple of other lovers beside Jerry. But I always insisted on the same ritual: my lover and I visited with him first then left his room to share private time in the adjoining guest room. I always made sure that both doors were wide open so that the sounds of our lovemaking were audible to him."

"The only time I ever helped with his care was straight after my lovers left. I went to him without showering and with a bowl of warm water to bathe him. I took off his clothes slowly, so he could feel the chill in the air. I washed him from head to toe hoping he would remember the great tenderness we once shared—the tenderness we had shared before he started disrespecting me. More often than not, tears welled up in his eyes and trickled down his cheeks. I allowed his tears to trickle for a while before wiping them away with a damp cloth. Only once or twice did I allow my tears."

"I found him dead one morning, after one of my lovers had left and I had gone in with my bowl. Another massive stroke, they said."

~~~~~

We were crossing Flat Bridge now; our final destination, Kingston, was less than an hour away.

~~~~~

"The thing is, I don't feel a stroke of guilt just a pained sadness: the same sadness I felt when he was fit and disrespecting me, the sadness I felt when I heard rumours about this or that woman, and the same pain I felt when he told me that his secretary was expecting his child. 'I will not be leaving my home,' he had said, 'but I will be caring for my child, and the child will come here sometimes.'"

"I still feel that same overwhelming pain and sadness. The only difference is that when he was alive I felt hope—hope that the pain would ease someday. I hoped that when he got older he would stop his bad behaviour and we would once again be happy together. Now, there is no hope. I go to his graveside hoping that one day I will get some relief."

6 A VIRGIN LIFE

A bird doesn't sing because it has an answer,
it sings because it has a song.
~ Maya Angelou ~

~~ One ~~

Martha lost her virginity on a beach in Grenada. It was the day after her fortieth birthday.

She was laying on a secluded part of Grand Anse Beach in the arms of a man almost twenty years her junior. It was dusk, and a soft blue-grey light was pushing aside the day. Impatiently night forced its way, bringing a scattering of stars and a crescent moon. The crashing sound from the loud and rhythmic waves made her sonorous breadth seem quiet. Only occasionally did her breathing lose its rhythm—flowing as silent, broken sighs.

She was amazed at the sensations she had experienced a few

minutes earlier. If she allowed it, there would be shame, but she brushed those feelings aside. She should be celebrating. It had happened at last, in the country she loved, although not with a man she knew or loved. What was once a badge of pride in her church had become an emblem for puzzlement, even ridicule. She could now throw off that badge, at least to herself and a few friends. There was no hope of her sexual liberation being part of her testimony in church.

The tangled footprints she had followed earlier, as they made their way to the secluded spot, were no longer visible—their secrets, like her secret, covered by the darkness.

Without warning, Leon untangled himself from her arms, stood up, and scooped her into his arms. His laughter mingled with her shrill shriek. He carried her into the sea as a mother carries her baby. She remained still as he brought her to a standing position and into a full embrace. She held him too, surprising herself again. He knew the water well; the darkness held no fear for him. She wondered how often he had performed this dance with foreign girls and what he wanted from her. There was no shortage of girls for a man like him.

~~~~~

Martha met Leon on the night before at a dance where she and her cousin Polly had gone to celebrate her birthday. For reasons Martha could not fathom, Leon gravitated towards her soon after she had arrived, and they spent most of the night dancing soca together. In their half conversations, Martha discovered that he was a soldier. Throughout the evening, Polly gave her other snippets of information: He was from a good family with money; he could have done anything but had ambitions to be an officer and then go into politics.

"Too young for you, though. I don't even think he's twenty-five yet," Polly had said.

His insistence that they meet the following afternoon had amused Martha. He insisted upon showing her the island. Assuring him that she might know the island better than him, she finally relented.

Tired as they were, the next afternoon he drove them to Saint Patrick, the parish on the northern tip of the island. The views across the sea were spectacular, and the clearly visible islands across the Caribbean Sea took her breath away. They went to Bathway Beach; he swam as she sat under the shade of an almond tree. Martha had not thought to bring her swimming costume. And even though Polly had cautioned her about chancing upon a beautiful beach and not being able to go into the water because she did not have her swimming costume, towel, and wrap with her, Martha was not prepared. Since there were only a few people in the distance on the beach minding their own business, Martha would have stripped down to her matching black bra and panties if she had known him better.

Leon took her to Sauteurs (the main town of Saint Patrick) and to Leapers' Hill, where legend has it that the Caribs jumped over the cliffs into the sea to avoid colonization by the French. They stopped at Punchbowl and Lake Antoine to see the volcanic cones and craters. The whole area was perfumed with the scent of nutmeg. They ate *Oil Down*, the island's national dish, and sipped sorrel spiced with nutmeg; then they enjoyed the slow drive back to St. George's, back to their spot on Grand Anse Beach.

~~ Two ~~

Leaving behind the shame of rejection, Martha left her home in Manchester when she was twenty years old. From the time they were in secondary school, most children (like her school friend Gloria) planned to relocate and work in London once they finished school, but not Martha. Manchester had everything Martha needed.

Most of Martha's ambitions centred on Peter, Pastor Grey's son. She could not remember a time when brethren in the church had not matched them together. As a young woman who held the favour of the pastor's son, Martha was envied by her friends and other girls in the church. Since there were fewer boys than girls and because members were not allowed to marry unbelievers, Martha took comfort knowing that there was a husband for her in the church.

Now, thinking about Peter was a door into Martha's consciousness that she tried to keep firmly closed. But occasionally a piece of music, a scent, the taste of something, or a sensation pried that door open—and with it unhealed wounds. How he must have ridiculed her silently, considered her the fool that she was. Twenty years after the episode, she still cringed at the thought.

Peter's mother, Sister Grey, loved Martha from the start and singled her out for favours. Sister Grey was a self-employed seamstress specializing in soft furnishings and fluffy, decorative bed sets. As far back as Martha could remember, Sister Grey showered her with presents, invited her to Sunday lunches, and spoke as if she were already her daughter-in-law.

After lunch on Sundays, as if on cue, family members always found things to do in other rooms of the house, leaving her with Peter alone in the living room. The Grey's living room was not unlike her family's living room: two rooms knocked through to form a large lounge; the usual floral wallpaper; a colourful, patterned carpet; a decorative, glass cabinet stuffed with special china and glasses; and religious symbols and pictures on the mantelpiece and walls.

The Grey's living room was dominated by a grand piano, not by a coffee table like most living rooms. Pastor Grey had bought the grand piano from a second-hand music shop in Wembley, while attending a convention. It had cost him twice its price to get it to Manchester. More often than not there was an acoustic guitar and a saxophone resting next to it in a corner of the room.

When Martha first started visiting Peter, who was six years her senior, she would sit on the far side of the room behind the piano where she was hardly visible; Peter would sit on the other side of the room and pretend to read his Bible while watching her steadily. Martha had a delicate appearance with her below-knee, flowery skirt, and long-sleeved, white blouse. Thinking that he might be expected to take control or direct their meetings, Peter would move and sit next to her.

His mother's awkward attempt at matchmaking amused him, and her choice of Martha as the match for him puzzled him. Yes, Martha was good looking and possessed a natural, unadorned beauty like other church girls. And Martha had a good singing voice and talent for playing the piano and guitar that few possessed, but Peter knew they were hardly a good match. Members of the church were aware, yet pretended not to notice that Peter only went to church to please his parents. Martha on the other hand was by everyone's reckoning a good Christian girl.

Peter sometimes imagined the shock on Martha's face if he were to tell her about the unsaved girls he saw outside the church—where they went and what they did. He knew that Martha would be appalled if she knew what he did with girls in parks, alleyways, and abandoned buildings in towns near Manchester and even in family homes when parents were out.

Peter's Sundays with Martha could never match the days he spent with the unsaved girls. Each Sunday with Martha was much the same as any other: stilted conversation under the pretence at reading and discussing the Bible.

One Sunday to Peter's surprise, Martha got up and started to play the piano. He watched with a smile. "Join me on the guitar," Martha said simply. Her quiet, soft voice and the sound that came from her fingers unexpectedly flooded him with desire. He was afraid to stand up, certain she would notice: *Have her eyes or mind ever wandered over my body? Are they on me now?*

After that day, little things that she did, how she spoke and moved and even turning to look at him caused a burning weakness in him. When she was in a room, regardless of who else was there or what else was going on, her presence overwhelmed the room and he had to fight to control his desire for her.

Their meetings, as neither of them called them dates, took on another level from that time. They could each play music by ear and invariably they would either start or end their musical ensemble with Martha's favourite hymn, "Great is Thy Faithfulness." Occasionally, he wrote and played a piece on the saxophone for her. Joyously, Martha would join him on the piano, which brought the family into the room for an impromptu singsong and sent Sister Grey into raptures of matchmaking success.

A few years later in his parents' living room, Peter proposed to

Martha: she was twenty; he was twenty-six. Their families met in that same sitting room to plan a wedding with a date less than six months away. "Everyone can see how much you two love each other, so we do not want to give any space to the devil by keeping you both from each other for too long," his mother counselled.

Less than a month before the wedding in the same sitting room, a grave Sister Grey and Martha's tearful mother sat Martha down for a talk. The night before, Martha had seen Peter in the same room. They had played music and sung together, and they had talked and laughed about their future together.

Since the announcement of their marriage in the church, she had allowed him to hold her and kiss her on the lips, not on her cheeks as had been the habit before the announcement. Just the night before, she had felt every muscle in his body as he held her to him while whispering in his ear that she did not know how she would be able to hold on for another day, let alone a whole month. "When I am weak, you have to be strong, and when you are weak, I have to be strong," she begged. "I want to be pure for you on the first night."

Now, like discordant music, the words of Sister Grey and her mother did not make sense. The women had just tearfully informed

Martha that Peter had made a girl pregnant with twins who was due to give birth any time now. Shocked and stunned, questions of disbelief flooded Martha's mind: *Who said? How do they know? Where is Peter? How can that be? That is a wicked lie.*

"Peter had made a terrible mistake," Sister Grey said. "He told me it only happened once seven months ago. He wanted to tell you, to beg your forgiveness, but he didn't have the courage. Because the babies are twins, she is having a caesarean at seven months. Peter's children will be born in a few days."

As Martha sobbed and her thin frame convulsed, her mother's strong arms were unable to succour her. Even as the words battered, Martha's mind raced ahead: she was running down the road, crossing the street, and turning the corner towards the road to her home; she saw the clothes she would pack, the taxi she would take, and the train she would take to her cousin Polly's flat in London. She embraced the darkness that loomed, accepting that darkness would forever be part of her life.

~~~~~

Many years later, old, arthritic, and bearing little resemblance to his old self in looks or fluency on the instruments he had so mastered, Peter would tell the story to his grandchildren of how he grew to love Martha. How he grew to adore her as she played the piano and he the acoustic guitar in his parents' living room in Manchester. How he never forgot or stopped loving her. How he would die haunted with regret. The grandchildren humoured him as much as he had enraged their mother, who had always blamed Martha for Peter's unwillingness to settle down with her.

The grandchildren were sure it was impossible to remember things that had happened so many years ago.

~~ Three ~~

Martha's family was not happy when she told them that she would be spending her fortieth birthday in Grenada, and not in Manchester with them. They had planned a surprise party for her, which they quickly rescheduled.

Not even her mother understood Martha's connection with the island she had left when she was four years old. Martha gave up trying to explain why she could not stay in England for more than a year without her Grenada fix, as she called it. She was the only one of her siblings who had been born on the island. Her eight siblings had been born in Manchester. The first sibling, Levi, was born a year after Martha and her parents had arrived in Manchester, then Sybil (a year after him), then four boys, and then two girls (a year and eighteen months apart). Martha did not expect her siblings to understand. They saw Grenada only as a glorious holiday destination, not the mecca of all that was good and right and perfect.

The Greens, who defined themselves first and foremost as Christians, were a significant family in their local Pentecostal church. There were a lot of factors that had to come together to turn a family into a church-family in the Church of Christ. For the Greens, these factors had not occurred all at once, but over many years, and they had not come without challenges. Every act of godliness—from the day in the mid-1950s that Mother Green first attended the Church of Christ in Manchester, to the births of her children, and through the children's achievements in school—was a significant step in the family's influence in the local and national church.

Levi eventually became the pastor everyone had said he should become. The other boys were talented musicians, and the younger girls (all except Sybil) were celebrated singers and musicians. They formed the Green Spirituals, a band not only known in their church but also known in other churches throughout the country. Martha was the most talented singer in the family; she regularly performed at gospel concerts, weddings, and other functions as a favoured soloist and pianist. She taught the piano on Saturdays and on some evenings after working in the bank.

Until that fateful day, no one doubted that the accomplished, tall, slim, and stunning Martha would marry Pastor Grey's son. When Martha was a young woman, brethren in the church unfairly compared her to the other young girls in the church, lamenting to the other girls why they couldn't be sincere, well behaved, good Christians like Martha. Even Sybil was sometimes asked why she couldn't be more like her sister.

At district and national conventions when other girls were seeking out boys and parading up and down the conference centre hoping that boys would notice them, Martha sat through the sessions and got up only during scheduled breaks. Her sister Sybil often mocked her: "I am glad I am not like you.... You must continue to act like a nun; otherwise, you are going to disappoint a lot of people."

"It's not about other people," Martha had told her sister. They had always shared a room, and more often than not, they did not get on. Sybil's sharp, venomous tongue was often too much for Martha.

When Martha was eighteen and Sybil was twelve, they had a memorable row. Martha found and read a few pages of Sybil's diary: *Everyone thinks we are so close, but we are light-years apart in every way.* Martha was upset that Sybil saw their relationship in that way, and Sybil was upset that Martha had the cheek to read her private diary. The row raged for hours as wounding words batted between them. Sybil in an uncaring tone (as was her nature about the effects of her words) ridiculed Martha's unsullied reputation: "You are frigid, and will die an old maid." *Frigid* a word she and her friends had recently explored about their hated Maths mistress.

Martha's virginity was a recurring topic in their rows over the years. Sybil tried to bully her sister into being more normal, as she called it. Sybil had even warned her about Peter: "You had better give in a bit to Peter. He will only go after other girls if you don't. He might even think you are a eunuch."

Martha, while standing by the door ready to leave their room, lost the strength in her legs and slipped to the floor. Only then did Sybil stop her verbal onslaught, sit next to her sister, hug her, and say, "I'm only joking. He loves you, and he'll wait—sorry, sorry, sorry."

~~ Four ~~

In London during the first few months after her corrosive shame, Martha often reflected upon her sister's prophetic words, and she blamed herself for what had transpired with Peter.

Only with Roselyn (a lecturer at one of the local colleges who Martha had met at church) was Martha able to articulate the depth of her wound. It was not easy for Martha to talk openly about her humiliation, but Roselyn was an easy person to talk to. Roselyn and Sybil were both born in the same month (both Scorpios), and they were both short and thin with penchants for speaking their minds. Roselyn, however, had a much greater consideration for the feelings of others than Martha's sister.

Roselyn got married to a chemistry teacher a few months after she and Martha had met. One evening while Roselyn's husband was out attending a parents' evening, Martha had dinner at Roselyn's home, and they talked about the relaxing of church rules. "Of course, I wasn't a virgin when I married," Roselyn had said.

"So you backslid and came back into the church after you married?"

Rose, as she liked to be called, laughed heartily. "I have not heard that phrase for years."

As she studied Martha's chiselled features, Rose continued: "I suppose I was always questioning the odd do-and-don't rules in our church but would never have battled with my parents about them when I was under their roof. Now? I go because I believe in God and because I like the people and the history of being brought up in it, but that's it. I do what I want. Perhaps I have always done what I've wanted." She paused, then added, "I was like you until I was eighteen and went away to university. Those divine men..." she said, with smiling eyes. "I had the will power of a saint in those days. For the first year, I did not go near any of them. All the girls in my hall (even the girls who used this or that religion as an excuse to live in an all-female hall) were in and out of bed with different men. I remember Angie from some extreme religious group or another. I used to go running in those days, and I caught David climbing out of her bedroom window early one morning." Rose laughed heartily, as she recalled the incident.

Martha was becoming impatient and wanted her friend to fast-forward the story. Martha was less interested in Angie and David and more concerned how her friend had become so flippant and casual about church rules—so free from the bondage of being brought up in a church with numerous antiquated and inexplicable doctrines.

Rose told Martha, "In my first year at university, I just blotted men out of my consciousness. I told myself the same old rubbish. I must be a virgin when I marry, and even worse, I can only date a man who is in the church. Then the second year came. I went to my first dance and met my first non-church-going boyfriend, George, and the rest is history. What I know for sure is that it's different with each man, in so many ways," she said, emphasising the *so*. "I would be mortified if I had not taken the opportunities that I was handed over the years. It even disappoints me that I was nineteen before I lost my virginity."

Martha listened for the ameliorating *Don't get me wrong, I did not sleep around*. But those words did not come. Rose continued eating and joking about her liaisons over the years and the double standards of those who preached chastity in the church. "Their conscience stopped dominating my actions when I was nineteen," Rose concluded.

Rose's perspective on the church and life, though shocking,

fascinated Martha. Martha had never imagined a church-woman like Rose. Foolish as she knew it sounded, Martha told Rose that she had always imagined that if she defied the doctrines of the church she would immediately feel the wrath of God. Rose was feeling no wrath, Martha thought, so why would she?

Martha found herself glancing at men again even imagining a time when she might give another man a chance. She liked spending time with Rose, her husband John, and their little girl, who was born a couple of years after they got married. It was as if her association with Rose lifted the darkness. Sometimes, when Martha rang Rose in the middle of a Saturday for a chat, she did not get a response. When she called back an hour or so later, Rose would laugh with the naturalness of someone long free and say: "John and I are spending the morning in bed. Charlene is with her grandparents. This week one set, the next week the other set. She is picked up in the morning or afternoon every weekend. That's why I am not at church some Sundays." Martha heard John's voice in the background and imagined that he was asking her to get back into bed.

~~ Five ~~

Martha had conflicting emotions when Sybil accepted a marriage proposal from a young Scot who was new to Manchester and not a member of the church. Martha thought that anyone whose family was not in the church could not possibly understand the church's strange rules and doctrines (or her family) and begged her sister not to marry him. But more than that, jealousy for her sister threatened to overwhelm Martha.

"You're only twenty," Martha protested. "It's mad."

"You are just jealous and sexually frustrated," her sister dismissively replied. "You were engaged to be married at the same age. Or have you blotted that history out of your mind."

Sybil was in London during a long bank-holiday weekend visiting Martha, and they decided to go shopping on Petticoat Lane. Martha did not want to miss church by shopping on a Sunday. Sybil said she would go on her own, but Martha protested, "You know I would not let you do that. You don't know London."

They spent Sunday afternoon shopping. Sybil bought t-shirts, a couple of handbags for herself, and shirts for her fiancée. On their way back to Martha's flat, Martha just missed colliding with a car that had run the lights.

"There is a message there somewhere," Martha stated. "This is a church day."

Sybil kissed her teeth.

Back in Streatham, Sybil told Martha more about Alistair. Martha asked why she had settled on him.

"You have not exactly been... what shall I say... reserved about other men who have shown interest in you," Martha said, hinting at her sister's flouting of the church's prohibition of close relationships with men before marriage.

"I choose to ignore that veiled criticism," Sybil said.

"No criticism. Just interested."

"I know you, Martha."

"OK, let's talk more about him when I come home next month," said Martha.

~~~~~

After six years of working at a bank, Martha bought a top-floor flat that overlooked Streatham Common. Being a bank employee, Martha got a four percent interest rate instead of the sixteen percent rate that others were paying. She was planning to invest in more properties as time went on. Martha had spent months fixing up her flat: stripping floral wallpaper, sanding floors back to the natural wood, and installing new light fittings. She hired a worker to plaster the walls, but she did the painting by herself. She had scoured second-hand shops for furniture finding a Victorian, four-poster bed, side boards, ornate occasional tables, and mirrors. She found a battered sofa, which she reupholstered like new, and a chaise lounge from the same period. On her annual trips to Grenada, she returned with prints and postcards, now gloriously framed and adorned on the walls.

London allowed Martha some freedom from the weight of Peter and all that surrounded him, but she hankered after the warmth and comfort of her childhood home in Manchester. Sybil brought the comfort of home with her when she visited Martha in London. And even though the sisters invariably disagreed or veered close to an argument for one reason or another whenever they met, Martha still begged her sister to visit at least once every other month. Sybil obliged, liking her sister's company but also secretly worrying and wanting to be with her to keep a check on her. Martha missed her family and the extended family of the church. She went home to Manchester during the months when Sybil did not visit her in

London.

Martha and Sybil were in their old bedroom on the very top floor of the house. Martha was home from London for the weekend to help with the wedding plans. Over the six years since Martha had left Manchester, she returned almost every month to visit her family but only occasionally went to church when she visited. She hated the pitying eyes. At first she blamed Peter's mother. Martha was convinced that Sister Grey knew all along what her son Peter had been up to and that she meant to sacrifice her to a life of pain. Then Martha blamed Peter's father, then Peter, then the church, and then everyone else including herself for being a fool.

Sybil reported to Martha that Peter had fully left the church and had joined the army. She had heard he was posted in Germany, did not marry the mother of his children, took care of his girls, and was with the mother of his children on and off. At first she sought to know everything she could about Peter's life, and Sybil provided information when she asked. But as time went on, Martha locked him away and prayed that she would not bump into him.

"I have to say, Sybil, it worries me that you saw men that you had no intention of marrying. Does Alastair know? He might find out and be disappointed."

Sybil laughed. "If by saw you mean slept with, how would that be his business?"

"Oh God, Sybil, of course, I do not mean that. I could never imagine that you would have defiled yourself in that way. Church girls don't sleep with men before they marry, but people have talked over the years, Sybil, about you getting too close to men with no intention of marrying them."

"Let them. I don't care. They are still talking about what happened to you, and you are the perfect Christian."

As soon as the words left her lips, Sybil apologized, "Sorry, sorry, sorry," and hugged her sister.

Martha shrugged. Sybil's words on that subject had long since ceased to wound her.

"Sybil, you are a virgin? Aren't you?" she blurted, surprising herself.

"How is that your business?" Sybil bellowed.

"My God!" Martha said.

Martha's mind drifted to Peter now as Sybil pontificated. There were no complete thoughts just flashing images of a piano, a saxophone, an acoustic guitar, and the sound of songs in the distance—tunes too far away to hear. His hands were the constant image: dark, strong, long fingers; thick knuckles; with crisscrossing and pronounced veins on the back of his hands. Occasionally, she wished she had played with his hands smoothing out the crisscrossing veins and kissing his thick knuckles. She also remembered his hugs in the days after his father had announced their engagement in the church. They were strong and protracted hugs. If she focused long enough, she could feel the muscles of his chest, where she had rested her cheek, and the caps of his knees against her legs. Would she ever feel those sensations again?

"It makes me laugh, how you church people treat sex as one of the deadly sins," Sybil proclaimed.

"You are in the church too, or you are supposed to be."

"You are twenty-six, Martha. Did what happened six years ago not teach you anything? You are the only one living by an outdated doctrine that some old fools concocted."

"That must be blasphemous," Martha said quietly. "Sex has to be within marriage, Sybil."

"Oh, well then!" Sybil said laughingly, before leaving to make tea.

Mother Green had heard their raised voices from the kitchen, but she could not make out what they were quarrelling about. She never intervened when they fell out, as no one could get a hair between them when they were getting on.

Sybil entered the kitchen humming, avoiding her mother's eyes and lopsided smile that she donned when she struggled to disguise her thoughts and emotions. Sybil knew her mother thought what only Martha had the courage to say. At least she would be married soon, and the family could finally put to rest their fear of Sybil's impending disgrace.

Mother Green was a gentle, quite, prayerful woman, who had taken emotional abuse and serial infidelity from her husband without complaining. God has a plan was her refrain. When Martha was sixteen, she could take it no longer and called the police saying her father had threatened to kill her mother.

"That is a barefaced lie and beyond belief," her father protested. "If I were that kind of man, I would have beaten her," he added.

In a fit of rage, Martha's father called Martha the mistake that should not have happened—a reference to her mother getting pregnant when they were both in high school in Grenada. He packed and left the home soon after the police left the house. He did not seek a divorce nor did their mother ask for one. He vowed never to enter the house again until his daughter was dead.

"And since I will die before you, that will never be" were his parting words to the family.

Over the years, Mother Green caught herself watching her first born, trying to read her mood and feelings much like a mystic who reads palms. In her heart of hearts, Mother Green was grateful to her daughter for bringing her disappointing marriage to an end.

Mother Green was frightened for her daughter, but she was not sure why. Mother Green's belief in God did not stop her from believing in her feelings and her dreams, and she had recurring dreams about Martha. Mother Green's dreams were very upsetting to her. She often woke with the feeling that the dreams took place in a foreign country, but she could never remember the details. Mother Green fasted and prayed for her daughter after each dream. As time passed, nothing caused her trepidation, so Mother Green ceased fearing for Martha but blamed her failed marriage on her anxieties about occurrences in foreign lands. Now, it was only fear that her daughter would never find love again that kept Mother Green awake sometimes.

Sybil drove her sister to the train station the following evening. The journey to London was long and tiring. Martha longed to be back in the solitude of her flat, alone with her broken dreams, her anxieties, and her fears. Finally home she dropped her bag and rushed to the bathroom as an unending stream of clear saliva sprung into and out of her mouth. As she spat, more saliva came; then more, as she violently and repeatedly vomited. Her stomach emptied; she retched and retched until she slumped to the floor exhausted. Levi was married; Sybil was getting married. She was the eldest. That night Martha suffered from insomnia, a condition that would plague her for years.

The church rules became more liberal over the years: female members could now wear jewellery and nail polish, did not have to wear a hat to church, and were allowed to don a bathing suit and swim in the same area with men. Women could even wear trousers, but marrying a man who was not in their church was still against the rules as was dating without an intention to marry.

Martha went up to Manchester again the following weekend to talk to her sister. Their daily phone conversations during the week had been strained. Martha could not hide or deny her jealousy. Martha so wished that it was she who was getting married, but she did not want her sister to think she did not wish her happiness.

The sisters were sprawled on the bed and stripped to their underwear. Seeking inspiration for the wedding dress and bridemaids' outfits she wanted a friend to make, Sybil had bridal magazines strewn about the bed. It was a Saturday evening, and the smell of their mother's cooking was intoxicating: beef soup (for that evening's meal) and chicken and fish (for Sunday lunch).

After church the next day, Martha and Sybil helped their mother cook the rice, roast the potatoes, steam the vegetables, and make the salad. There would be jelly with fruit salad and ice cream for dessert.

After dinner while their mother and siblings were out at band or choir practice, Sybil turned to Martha and said, "I know I disappoint you. You think marrying an unbeliever is not becoming of a Christian, but your take on Christianity has never been mine."

"I try not to judge you, Sybil. You are a good person. Everyone loves you."

Sybil smiled. "They are wary of me, you mean. They are afraid I will bite their heads off if they upset me."

"That is only one side of you. You are a lovely person. He is lucky to have you."

After moments of silence, Sybil said, "I know people in our church think you can only be a true Christian if you are in our church. But Alastair is a believer, and that is important to me and to any children we may have. He believes in God, and he knows and loves my family—our family, our rock. Martha, I know you love me and that we have a strong family, so I am not worried about anything and you shouldn't either. We will always have each other and our family—the only place we will find unconditional love."

Martha and Sybil hugged tightly and for a long time.

Later, Martha got her guitar and played; they sang together well into the night.

~~ Six ~~

After Martha met Barry at a training workshop, Rose was the only person Martha told. It was the first time she had dated since Peter. "It has taken me ten years to get over a man; that must be a record," Martha confessed to her tender-eared friend.

Rose, surprised that she was seeing someone who was not in the church, encouraged Martha to take it slowly. "I'm not bothered as you know, after all I am married to an unbeliever, but you have always expressed such strong feelings."

"I know, I know" was all Martha found to say.

Martha called Rose several times during the week to talk about Barry's every action: what he said and did, where he took her, and what he did when they were out. When talking to Rose, Martha was light-hearted and relaxed; giggles and laughter punctuated her words.

"Take is slowly, Martha," Rose advised, and not just once.

Rose feared hurt and trouble ahead. "Are you sure you are the one in control? The expectations of unbelievers are different from those of men who have been indoctrinated in the church."

Martha commented on her use of *indoctrinated*. They laughed about it.

"If it gets serious, I will bring him into the church," Martha said, with certainty. "He invited me to stay the night after we went out yesterday evening. Can you believe it? I hardly know him."

"That's what I mean, Martha. In general, people don't think of sex as you do, Martha. It's no big deal for most people. It's just fun."

A few weeks later, Martha called Rose and told her that Barry ended their friendship. Rose listened intently, fearing Martha would blurt out *I knew it couldn't last.*

"He asked me to stay the night again, so I told him I was a virgin. He said he could not take that responsibility. Can you believe that?"

Rose made consoling remarks and suggested that perhaps next time she should not say that she was a virgin.

Though piqued, Martha was not hurt; nothing could touch the hurt of ten years ago. The experience had solidified her views that finding a good man was all too much work. Rose was right. If there was a next time, she should not behave as if she was special.

The men in the church were no longer a possibility for Martha. She did not notice them anymore, and they seemed to put her in the same category as the old married women or the no-hope-of-marriage group who had had children outside of marriage or who had not managed to shift one rumour or another about something they had done years ago.

As she got older (and wiser), Martha became more confident around men in the church, but the chasm of scepticism by men in the church towards her remained. She joked with them and found it easier to engage them in conversation, but that was where it ended.

Martha could not help fixating on what she considered their nasty habits. She often watched the men fidgeting surreptitiously in church. But it was what they did with their hands that made her wretch: digging in their ears, scratching their head, picking their nose or teeth, and pulling at their crotch. No doubt women did similar things, she thought, but she only noticed men doing these gross things, and it repulsed her. She could not imagine allowing the hands from such men to touch her. When she was in church, she took to offering her left hand, sometimes an elbow, when they reached out to shake her hand. She kept a solution of Dettol and water in a spray bottle in her car and sprayed her hands as soon as she left church. When she got home, she washed her hands furiously with antibacterial soap.

Brother Russell was a case in point. Not long after Martha had moved away from Manchester, she started hearing rumours about how Brother Russell belittled and demeaned his wife. One night after service the rumours became fused with reality. As Brother Russell piled passengers into his car and other members shuffled and piled into the few cars that members owned, Sister Russell was left behind to beg a lift or take the bus. Brother Russell was known to openly scoff at his wife in business meetings when she expressed an opinion he did not like. Everyone, it seemed, sided with Sister Russell and pilloried Brother Russell behind his back. When the young people wanted an example of a man who they did not want their future husbands to be like, Brother Russell was the example.

Sister Russell died from a sudden brain haemorrhage one night soon after she had arrived home from church. The church grieved her loss. She had been one of the first members of the church and one of the first new immigrants in their branch to train as a state-registered nurse. Rumours grew that Brother Russell's anger towards his wife stemmed from the fact that he had wanted a child, and she had not been able to have one. And more, there was a crescendo of gossip that she had left a large sum of money to Brother Carter, a backslidden member of the church. Apparently, Sister Russell and Brother Carter had been lovers for many years, and Brother Russell had known about this all along.

Less than a month after his wife's death, Brother Russell knocked on Martha's door. The loud series of knocks on the front door startled Martha. She had just arrived home from work, dropped her bag, and washed her hands and was getting ready to prepare a salad. She ran down the stairs, opened the door, and found Brother Russell.

"Brother Russell!" she said, not disguising her frown. Only once had she had a man from the church in her flat and that had been for the usual house-warming prayer meeting. She occasionally had women to dinner on Sundays, but no one had ever dropped by without an invitation.

"I would like an urgent word with you, Sister Green," he said.

Not able to imagine what urgent words he could possibly have for her, she stood firm while holding the door ajar as he stood on the threshold.

"I need to come in," he said, gently pushing the door back and stepping inside.

"I am sorry, Brother Russell, but my flat is a mess. I have just got in from work."

He hesitated for a moment, as if he had not rehearsed that possibility.

"That is not a problem for me," he said.

"OK, turn right at the top," she said, as they climbed the stairs.

For some reason, she found his thunderous footsteps and heavy breathing irritating as he manoeuvered the steep steps. The dining room and kitchen were straight ahead and messier than the sitting room on the other side of the flat.

Although Martha was relatively new to that branch of the church, she had grown to like Sister Russell; and for a moment, she imagined that his visit was somehow connected to her. She would not offer tea so as not to extend the visit. She showed him to the armchair, and she sat on the edge of the sofa looking steadily at him.

"I have come to ask for your hand in marriage," he said, without ceremony. The words rolled off of his tongue as if he was asking to put his bag on the table. To her ears, the words were a disparate unconnected jumble. It was moments before she connected the words and understood what he was saying. She laughed.

"I know it may seem too early to you, as Sister Russell has just died, but I have been watching you since you came to the church, and…"

"Brother Russell, I do not want to say something I will regret or be rude to you, so please do not say anything else. Please leave now."

"Sis Green, you are not a young woman and…"

She stood up. "You are older than my father. Leave now. Please."

She followed him to the bottom of the steps; then she opened the front door. He turned for a moment as if to speak again. She shook her head and shut the door. She heard him close his car door; then she heard him drive away.

She heard other cars make their way over the newly installed speed humps. Periodically, she heard the voices of people walking past the flat going home from work to their families. She stood by the front door for minutes then slumped to a seated position on the bottom step. She didn't move until she was numb and cold.

~~ Seven ~~

Over the next few years, Martha vacillated between crippling fear and stubborn resolve. She feared that she would grow old alone and there was nothing she could do about it; she was steadfast in her resolution to find ways to make the most of her life. She sought distractions in evening classes. She took classes in French polishing, sewing, and French. She even attended a year of classes in basic car mechanics. Those distractions were contrived, others fortuitous.

One evening after work she got talking to a Trinidadian on the platform at Waterloo Station. Jenny's preferred waiting spot was next to her preferred spot, and Martha noticed that she got off at Balham, one stop before hers. Frequent delays and cancellations of the trains encouraged polite conversation until it seemed like they were longtime friends. Jenny liked soca music (and so did Martha) and invited Martha to a soca party in West London. Soon they were meeting up to dance to soca music at dance halls and clubs around London and sometimes at clubs as far away as Birmingham and Sheffield. Jenny was married; so were her friends. They were all longtime married, and none of Jenny's friends seemed to mind Martha around their husbands. It was normal in the group to swap husbands on the dance floor. Dancing was one church rule that had changed over the years. When Martha was a teenager, church members were only allowed to dance in the spirit in church. Back then it was an abomination to God to attend dances and dance to secular music.

After her cousin Polly migrated to Grenada, Martha had an even greater reason to visit her beloved island each year. And like soca dancing with Jenny and her married friends, visiting Grenada gave Martha reasons to be expansive in her life. So even without the husband and family she so desired, Martha's life still had some wide-open gaps of happiness and fun.

In Grenada, Martha befriended Polly's housekeeper, Nerri, and her only son, Keith. Martha's friendship with Nerri and Keith came to fill the gaps that her hobbies and interests could not fill. In the evenings after school, Keith came to Polly's house to wait for his mother. His tenderness towards his mother touched Martha. Martha often saw Keith hugging and kissing his mother, and Keith was keen to help his mother carry her belongings, lightening her load, on the long walk home.

Nerri was married, but her husband's stroke had left him disabled and unable to share financial responsibility for the family. A few years after Martha met the family, she heard he had died.

Martha found herself taking more and more responsibility for the family's wellbeing, especially for Keith, the youngest. Martha paid for his uniform, books, and private tuition in English and Maths. Martha also encouraged Keith to take up the piano and guitar. She purchased both instruments in England and shipped them to his family. Each year she looked forward to seeing his progress in school and music. Every year when she visited Grenada, she brought along a barrel of clothes and books, requiring extra time for her to clear customs upon arrival. Once in Grenada, Martha made time for Keith and his family helping with home repairs and ensuring that his mother had any medical treatment she needed.

When Keith passed his Common Entrance for high school, Martha opened an investment account for him. Martha added to the account monthly and told his mother that he would be able to access the account when he was thirty years old. As he grew older and excelled in school and college, Martha was effusive in her pride about him. And in her will, Martha named him her sole beneficiary for all she owned in Grenada. Her possessions in England were left to her nieces and nephews.

When Martha was forty visiting Grenada for her birthday, Keith was eighteen years old and about to enter teachers' college. Martha had recently purchased a large house in Surrey and was renting her flat in Streatham. During this visit to Grenada, Martha purchased a plot of land and laid the foundation for a home before she returned to England. She told her family she planned to return to Grenada for good when she turned fifty.

Over the next ten years, Martha's passionate relationship with Leon, endured their annual, eleven-months-long separation and Leon's life with the wife he married soon after he and Martha had met when she was forty and he was twenty-five years old. Martha did not know where the feeling of not caring about Leon's fiancée (and later, wife) came from, but bothered she was not. She had no intention of flaunting their relationship and harboured no feelings of jealousy or possessiveness.

Martha and Leon spoke on the phone several times a week when she was in England, and when she visited for the month-long, annual visit, she saw him every day, if not every night. Martha did not ask and Leon did not tell her anything about the woman he had married, but Leon did introduce Martha to each of his three sons who were born during the first three years of his marriage. During Leon's wife's pregnancies, Polly would comment, "You have changed so much." Martha knew she did not mean for the better.

Only Polly and Rose (who was now divorced and living with her two daughters) knew the extent of her relationship with Leon: about the two lives he led and the part Martha played in them. When Sybil visited the island and saw them together, Sybil said she could not believe that they were just friends, as Martha had insisted, but Sybil did not belabour the point. Over the years, the rest of Martha's family eventually met Leon when they went to Grenada on holiday. Keith was also always around to show off about and distract them.

Sybil, Alistair, and their children migrated to Jamaica about a year after Martha relocated to her beloved Grenada. Alastair had a contract with a telecommunications company. Sybil joked that her lot was to live the life of a stay-at-home, ex-pat mother in Montego Bay.

After Sybil had been in Jamaica for a year, Martha visited her sister. They lived in a townhouse at the Lagoons in Montego Bay.

"You have your private beach. How idyllic can you get?" Martha commented.

"I know. It is divine."

Next to their property was a private mooring. Sybil and Martha watched as a boat was launched from the mooring and made its way into the expanse of the turquoise waters.

"The lagoon area is sheltered and protected," Sybil told Martha. "When there is a hurricane the yacht club across the road brings their boats here for shelter."

"It is divine. But you must be bored with the children at school."

"I don't have a work permit, but I am keeping myself busy. I'm learning Spanish and taking piano lessons.

Martha snickered.

"I knew you would laugh."

"You were adamant; you were not going to learn when we were little."

"It was too much. Green Spirituals, for God's sake. Everyone was into music. I wanted to be different."

"You were. Believe me."

"So, Martha, how is your business going? Importing fish into an island that has more fish than water doesn't seem to be a wise choice."

"It's not easy, but the fish I get, salmon and tuna, are not caught locally. Business is okay. But as you know, I don't depend on it totally. I do have my early-retirement pension."

"How is Keith? Lucky man!" Sybil exclaimed.

"He is twenty-eight now, you know. Can you believe it?"

"Amazing, the son you never had."

"Actually, yes, it feels like that. He is head of the science department in his school and still gives piano lessons. I think he has ambitions to migrate to Canada. It will be good for him to experience life in another country. I hope he finds a deserving girl."

"Is he serious with anyone?"

"I have met a few girls over the years, but I don't think he's ready to settle down. And the great thing, he has not fathered any stray children. I'm proud of him for that too."

For the first time in years, Martha asked about Peter. "Have you heard anything about Peter recently?" Sybil reported that she had seen him a few months before she had left England.

"He has aged a lot, and he has rheumatoid arthritis," Sybil reported. Sybil watched for her sister's reaction, then continued: "He lives alone. Never married or settled for long with the mother of the twins. Lives for his girls and grandchildren, I heard."

"Isn't it odd, how in over thirty years we have only met up a few times," Martha grimaced. "And we had hardly anything to say to each other when we did."

"It's been a long time, Martha. And he did write you that letter."

"I know. What a fool I was."

"No, just naïve."

"Never read it."

"Do you regret that?"

"Of course. I imagine it is like having a stillborn child and not looking at it or asking what sex it is. I imagine you would regret that forever," Martha said.

"You silenced him for good."

"I used to laugh at old women reminiscing, thinking they could not remember things that happened when they were young. In fact, I used to laugh at those women in the church."

"Me too."

"One remembers, though."

"I know."

"Scents, sensations, emotions—I loved him, you know. I did not know how much then. I wish now that I had gone the whole way. He may not have gone with her."

"Or he may. What you did or did not do had nothing to do with how he behaved. But I can imagine that you have missed him over the years. Missed knowing what could have been." Then Sybil gasped a long sigh. "Memories can be wonderful though, Martha."

"I know."

~~ Eight ~~

After a roundabout trip to Grenada from Jamaica via Port of Spain, Martha arrived back in St. George's exhausted. For the life of her she could not work out why it was so hard to travel between

Caribbean islands.

She had received several text messages from Keith while she was in Jamaica. He needed to see her urgently. She had called Polly who hesitated but finally said that there were rumours about Keith being in debt. Questions such as *what*, *with whom*, and *why* raced through Martha's mind. Polly could not say.

Wanting to spend time with Leon when she got home, Martha was irritated that Keith was waiting for her outside her house when she and Leon arrived from the airport. Leon said he would give her time to visit with Keith and rest. He would come back the following evening.

Martha took her time showering. She could not believe what Polly had said. Her instincts were to tackle him without waiting to hear anything he had to say. There is no way he needed anything. He worked full-time, and Martha still paid his mother's utility bills (a kindness Martha had taken on so Keith could not use the absence of light as an excuse for failing to do his homework). Martha also paid for medical insurance for his mother and bought both of them clothes at least twice a year. They had no rent to pay since he and his mother now lived in a house and on land left to them by foreparents.

His siblings had migrated abroad, and Martha knew they sent remittances to their mother. *How could he be in debt?*

Keith was impatient to speak to her. He saw her as a second mother, and he was careful to show her respect, even though her wish to control him irritated him. He was not a child now—not like when desperation made him do whatever Martha wanted or when his mother warned him to behave for fear that if he did not Martha would withdraw her favours.

"How are your students getting on?" Martha inquired.

"Teaching piano is not for me, you know, Aunty Martha. I want to stop. Besides, I do enough teaching at school."

"Oh," Martha sighed.

Her disappointed look angered him. He was twenty-eight; she could not control him or tell him what to do.

"When will you stop?"

"I did when you left."

"I thought you said you wanted to stop. You mean you have stopped. There is a difference. So, what about the students who are doing exams?"

He did not respond.

"If I had stopped my responsibility to you, where would you be now?" She always asked that of him.

How long would she hold what she had done for him over the years over his head? Would he have to be grateful for the rest of his life? Be her little lackey, her thank-you boy?

She did not like his tone or his attitude, and she did not recognise the expression on his face. In all the years she had known him, she had never seen that intense, fixed expression—as if uncontrollable rage had welled up inside him.

"Let's discuss your students another time. What did you want to see me about? I am incredibly tired. And I want to give my mum a ring."

"OK, sorry." His tone and expression softened.

He had only met Mother Green in person a few times, but from the time he was young, she had taken a special interest in him: speaking to him on the phone (like everyone else in the Green family) and sending along gifts with Martha for him when he was young.

"Give Mama Green my love," he said, as he listened to Martha's tired voice.

"How is the blood pressure, Mum? I hope you are taking your

tablets."

Mother Green wanted to know about Sybil and whether she was in a safe area in Jamaica.

Martha reassured her mother: "You cannot take on the bad press that they give Jamaica, you know. It is nice, and nothing bad happens where she lives. It's wonderful, actually. I would live there."

After she got off the phone, Keith seemed to have relaxed and asked if he could speak to her the following day. She was glad and suggested they make a day of it and take a long drive somewhere. She had taught him to drive and left her jeep for him to use whenever she was in England.

When she had first started helping his family, she often took them on picnics to the nearby park. Martha and Keith's mother used to sit together looking at the cliffs as the children played. As they sat by the cliffs, Martha had talked about her plans for Keith: music lessons, schoolwork, books she needed to buy, and what she would put in the trunk for him and his family after she returned home to England. The warmth of these memories eased Martha's tiredness and her concern about what was on Keith's mind.

The ceiling and floor fans were on, the windows and doors were open, but Martha was still drenched with perspiration. She took another shower. The hot water (heated in a tank under the house) took some time to get to her. She shivered under the cool of the water as she waited for the warm water to come through. She lathered her wash sponge with Pears soap, which she so loved the smell of, and allowed the warm water to flow over her. She turned the dial to cold and lingered under the cool water for a few moments shivering but enjoying the cool. She knew that the coolness would not stay with her for long after she was out of the shower, before her body was once again engulfed in the sweltering night heat of St. George's.

After her shower, Martha called Sybil to tell her she was home safe and would speak to her for longer the following evening. Martha feared she would not be able to sleep. Try as she might, the insomnia that had started years ago no longer yielded to the various remedies: herbal medication, essential oil, and even yoga just before bed. Martha had told Sybil that she hoped her extreme tiredness would do the trick in overcoming her insomnia.

Martha opened her cases and shared out the gifts she had bought for Keith and his mother. She could not resist buying and giving them things she thought they would like when she travelled. Sybil was right. Keith was the child she desired. From the moment she had met him and his family, she had warmed to him and often felt that she could not love a child she bore any more than she loved him. It was well past two in the morning when she finally fell asleep.

Keith arrived early in the jeep. He was calm and quiet, unlike his normal garrulous self. Martha, feeling surprisingly rested, was keen to hear what he wanted to say and suggested they talk over breakfast. Keith had eaten and asked if they could go for the long drive she had promised and talk then. She packed a cooler with soft drinks, water, and ice.

"Let's drive to Saint Patrick, to Leapers' Hill," Martha suggested. "I know it's a long drive, but I can sleep as you drive if tiredness comes over me. We can call your mother to join us for lunch later. There are some nice places to eat around there. We can grab a bite after you have told me your big secret." Her attempt to make light of their impending talk was not successful.

"OK," he said.

She fell asleep soon after they left St. George's, and she woke to her protracted sigh as he parked the jeep.

"I need you to give me the money that you have been saving for me. It's due to me in two years anyway. I need it now."

They had just pulled up and parked as near to the cliffs as they could safely stop. The contrast between the calm, deep-turquoise sea and the jagged rocks sometimes made her fearful—such beauty and ugliness juxtaposed. She would peep over as she always did, not too close but enough to remind her of the thin line that separated safety from danger.

"What?" she said, momentarily confused. "What money?"

Then the fog induced by her nap cleared. He was referring to the investments she had made for him that were due when he was thirty years old. They had not left the car, but they had immediately flung the doors open to allow the breeze.

"What do you need it for? You are working."

"Aunty Martha, I would not ask if it was not important."

She sighed heavily. He had never asked her for anything over the years. She wondered what he had got himself into. She asked him why he needed the money so urgently.

"Are you in trouble?" she asked. She did not want to let on about the rumours she had heard from Polly. It was a small island.

"I just need it. You know I am not wasteful."

"I know you are sensible."

Despite all the sleep, she suddenly felt expended as if something had sucked all the energy from her. There was no way she could access the funds without penalty, but she could offer to lend him what he needed. The open door was not letting in enough air to cool her, so she tried to leave the jeep, to go stand in the open. The park was quiet; there was no one in sight.

As Martha turned to go, Keith grabbed her arm. She turned towards him sharply with knitted brow.

"Keith, what are you doing? Are you ill? Is something wrong with you? Tell me."

Instead of speaking, he stretched over her and pulled the door shut closing his door too.

"What are you doing? What is going on?"

"I need the money. You must give it to me today."

Furious now, she made to open the door. It was then that she felt the first blow to the side of her face. Open-mouthed and panicked, she impulsively flung her hand to hit him. He held her arms with one hand and hit her again with the other. She felt an incredible pain in her eye, then in her head. She had always thought it was a figure of speech when people spoke of seeing stars—now she knew differently. She screamed and tried to grab his hands. She tried to plunge her long nails into his eyes and, at the same time, get out of the car. She managed the lock then stumbled out of the car. Keith was by her side in no time grabbing her by the arm.

"Keith, Keith, please. What are you doing? Why? What are you doing?" she pleaded.

"If I can't get it while you are alive, I will surely get it once you're dead."

She fought him. Mustering all the strength she could, she tried to pull away from him at the same time screaming for help. Only her panicked screams came back to her. She caught sight of his face. That was not the face of the person who she had fed, educated, pampered, and adored. She closed her eyes and realized that he was pulling her towards the edge of the cliff. Panic and fear renewed her strength. Using her legs and arms, she tried to stop the momentum of her body towards the edge of the cliff. But she was no match for his youth, his strength, his fury.

Realizing she had done everything she could (and had lost) and knowing there was nothing she could do, Martha felt overwhelmed—like a tsunami hitting high tide. She let herself go into the force of his arms as he dragged her. The grass and stones grazed and then tore her skin. Her body burned as if he had put fire to her skin. *How real is this nightmare?*

Then, as if lowered into a soothing balm, the pain abated taking with it her fear, her pain, and her panic. She heard singing from above as if it were her own voice. She saw her fingers glide expertly over the keys of a piano. She heard the acoustic guitar. *Great is Thy faithfulness, O God my Father. There is no shadow of turning with Thee.*

Keith stopped and looked around. There was no one in sight. If there had been someone watching, they would have thought he was about to leave her as she was: her body bruised and limp, spots of blood breaking through her skin, her head suspended over the cliff's edge.

Martha in her half consciousness took in the rocks below—the waves drumming against the rocks making music sweeter than any human could compose. She felt his firm hands slide under her lifting her clean off the ground. She knew that soon she would be resting on the jagged edges below. She saw her family: her mother, her siblings, and even her father was there waiting to re-enter their home. Her family would be the rocks upon which she would fall: her mother with her lopsided smile, her brothers and sisters playing in the band heralding her descent, and Sybil (irascible, but as always) suffused with unconditional love.

7 EMPRESS

Only the dead have seen the end of the war.
~ Plato ~

~~ Andrew ~~

Corrine shouted the usual cautions to her son as he was about to leave the house: "Be sensible on the bus, Andrew. Listen to your teachers in school. Put your head to your studies. Girls won't be going out of fashion, so they can wait. And good luck for the match today. Sorry, but you know I can't go to watch it."

As he approached the front door to leave for school, Andrew wondered, and not for the first time, if his mother had a camera positioned at the door. *How else could her timing be so perfect?* Every day as soon as he raised his hand to unlock the door, she would call the same words from her bedroom as she was getting ready for work.

"Love you too, Mum. And I know you love me," he said under his breath, not loud enough for her to hear. He wished instead he could say, *Not hard to be sensible on the bus. Most of the teachers are not worth listening to, but what choice do I have? I'm okay with you not being at the match. I have my fans. And, it's the girls who won't leave me alone.* He played with his chin as the last thought lingered—and with it a grin.

Andrew was tall for his sixteen years, already well over six feet. He loved sports, especially football, and playing sports gave him a well-toned frame. His body looked older than his age, but not his face. He had a young-looking face, which he inherited from his father. His smiling eyes and contagious smile made his face attractive, invariably inviting a second look.

Andrew smiled all the time even when being reprimanded. When Andrew misbehaved at primary school and his mother was summoned by the teachers, she would tell them that he was born with that smile. The teachers eventually came to know that he was not being rude and made allowances for his perpetually cheerful face.

Andrew took his time walking to the bus stop; his characteristic dawdling suggested that going to the bus stop for school was the last thing he wanted to do. But he looked forward to the day: Maths and

English, his best subjects, then the after-school match. He called "good morning" to his neighbour who was on her veranda breastfeeding and recited the same to everyone he passed within earshot.

Andrew met Courtenay at the corner. Courtenay also lived in the community. Taking the bus together was a tradition that started in primary school because their working parents could not take them.

"Hi."

"Morning," Courtenay responded. "I was too tired to do Miss Burke's homework last night, Bro."

"Detention for you, then."

"Not staying for any detention. We have the match after school. Will have to copy yours on the bus."

Andrew groaned, dug in his bag for his book, and gave it to his friend. "Just make sure you change some of the workings out and some of the answers too."

"Thanks."

The bus came on time, and Andrew and his friend piled in with the other schoolchildren: all wearing competitive uniforms, all heading for various schools in and around Montego Bay. Workers heading in the same direction preferred not taking the bus because of so many schoolchildren. Workers making good time waited for route taxis. Workers pressed for time gritted their teeth, boarded buses with the schoolchildren, and tried hard to ignore petty squabbles, obviously played-out rivalries, and seething contentions between the boys and girls.

Andrew's father had died of prostate cancer four years earlier when Andrew was nearly twelve years old. The shock, pain, and failure to understand how such a thing could happen never left him. Andrew sat for weeks after the funeral babbling in corners while holding one or another of his father's belongings. Corrine took him to the doctor who told her to give him time and to get him involved in as many activities as possible. That's how his passion for basketball and soccer started. But she didn't want him to carry on with sprinting as his father had so loved.

Andrew had shown a flair for sprinting almost as soon as he was old enough to walk, and his father had dreamt of him being a track star. Andrew's father boasted in the office where he worked as an insurance broker that his son was as fast as lightening.

Andrew's father often took his son to the beach where they ran up and down. He would challenge his son: "Bet you can't run faster than me." Andrew's father had represented his parish at track and field meets in the hundred-metre sprints when he was in high school. Until Andrew was about nine years old, his father had held back, but after age nine he had to make an effort to keep up with his son. Corrine would tease him when they were alone in their room: "You should be ashamed. You let the little baby boy beat you in the race."

"Wey you taking 'bout? You no see me mek him win?" He would smile to himself visualizing his son setting records in Jamaica and abroad.

The bus, packed to capacity, arrived at the bus park in Montego Bay. Andrew and Courtenay were in the back, so it was minutes before they could get off. As was usual in the mornings, they continued their journeys to school by taking different means. Courtenay, pleading that the sun was too hot for him to walk, went to the taxi stand; Andrew walked the rest of the way to school. It took Andrew fifteen minutes to walk to school. He told his friend and other boys from school who he met along the way that he liked walking because it gave him time to think. Because of this and out of sympathy for having lost his father, he earned the nickname Thinker.

The nickname followed him to the football field where it became Tinker among those who thronged the public parks. At the fields where the boys' teams played, Tinker was recognized as the one to watch.

In the evenings, Andrew walked back to the bus stop and met up with other athletes from the soccer or basketball team who were going his way after practice or with Courtenay, if they went straight home. Occasionally, if their times synced, Andrew met his mother at the hairdressing salon she owned in the centre of town, and they would go home together in a taxi rather than on the bus.

"Thinker, see you at practice at lunchtime," Courtenay called after him, as Andrew turned out of the bus park and into the alley that led past the gas station and onto the main road.

~~ Corrine ~~

Corrine glanced at the wall clock in her bedroom. If she didn't get out of the house soon to get the route taxi, she would be late.

She and Rainsford had purchased the shop after the previous owner had fallen into financial difficulties. The monthly maintenance was not too onerous, even though the water and electricity charges were high; she managed by letting six chairs in the shop.

Corrine was glad they had had the foresight. Neither of them had imagined that less than two years later he would be diagnosed with cancer and dead. She somehow managed to make ends meet: he had left her a small life-insurance policy and she owned her house left to her by a great aunt. But without her business, life would have been hard.

She had awoken with her left eye leaping; now tears were springing from it. Irritated, she wiped them with the back of her hand. *Why do they still come so suddenly and without warning? Surely, they should be dry by now.*

She sat on the bed, her breathing fitful. She ran her hand over the covers as if to smooth them out. She was remembering the day her husband had slipped away—with Andrew lying in the crux of his arm. He was weak, slipping in and out of consciousness, but aware enough of his son. He wanted Andrew to be there as he took the final breath he knew would not be long in coming. Somehow he mustered enough strength to stroke his son's arm and whisper words hardly audible—words meant to bolster his son for the days ahead without him.

Corrine loved the relationship she had had with her husband. She had always prayed, *If he can love only one of us, let him love our child.* As long as he always loved Andrew, she would be at peace—at home or abroad. Happily for her, he had enough love for them both.

She had wanted to send Andrew away to stay with her parents when the end approached. His parents had not left Corrine and their son's house from the time they were told the end was near: his mother's face bathed with her tears and perspiration; his father in a daze, confounded at the suddenness of it all. One of the nurses had said to them, "Let the young boy face the trauma now. It will be hard, but harder if you exclude him."

When the vehicle from the funeral home came to take his body away, it had not been easy. The morticians had been patient, slowly coaxing him and prizing his little hand away from his father's neck. He hadn't cried that day or on the day of the funeral. He had hardly spoken and only picked at his food. She was sure he would get ill. It wasn't until weeks after the funeral that he had started to cry, and then he could not be consoled.

"I hope you don't think I'm being disloyal or that I will let anyone take first place over your son," she whispered, as she looked at one of the pictures of Rainsford that sat on the chest of drawers. She was talking about Ancel whom she had finally agreed to give a chance, as she called it. She had been seeing him for a couple of months. They stole time to be alone on some Wednesdays, when the shop was closed, and a few times when Andrew was playing soccer.

Ancel had finally come to terms with her way of doing things. It was her way, she had told him, or there would be no relationship. He could come to her home, but he could not stay the night, and there was absolutely no intimacy when her son was in the house, she had insisted.

"I am the one who normally gives the rules," he had said seriously.

She had been serious too. *You are not a need in my life*, she was thinking as he spoke, *just a want.*

"OK, you women with your own business and money. I will never understand how time changed up on me," he had said poutingly. This was his way of yielding.

She had noticed him go in and out of the house across the street for a few months before she acknowledged his gaze. Everyone living in her community had some history there or history with someone who lived there. Complete strangers were unusual, especially since the community had changed from a desirable, sought-after place to live to one sandwiched between informal squatter dwellings. He must be a confident person, she had mused. She often watched him through her kitchen window as he manoeuvered his overly large car (too flashy for the humble area) into the drive. The house had been on the market since its owners moved abroad, so she imagined he had bought rather than rented.

Corrine was convinced he tried to waylay her one day as she turned the corner from her road and noticed his car parked in front of his house. He had offered her a lift. She had refused, of course. A couple of weeks later, he came to her gate and introduced himself.

"I was foolish the other week. No sane woman would have accepted a lift from a strange man like me."

"I am Corrine. And the tall, young man over there is my son Andrew," she had said, as she turned to look at the group of boys who were playing ball in her garden at the side of the house picking out Andrew.

"I know you have your protection," he had said smiling. "I will watch myself from now on."

She had been amused by his words, but she still refused the lift he offered her a few days later.

"I have my routine," she had said. "I am comfortable taking my taxi."

Later that week he had turned up at her shop for a head massage from the barber. *It's a small city*, she had said to herself. *It must be a coincidence.*

After she finally decided to go for a meal with him, she had asked him how he happened to walk into her shop.

"It's easy to find anyone in this place if you want to."

Ancel was not the talkative type, but she eventually found out that he was not born in Jamaica but rather England. He was twice divorced he had told her without ado: his two ex-wives and five children all lived in London. He had said that he had been in and out of Jamaica over the years.

"How do you make your living if you are in and out?" she had inquired.

"I have a shipping company in London. People move back to Jamaica almost every day, and plenty of people ship barrels, especially at Christmas. I'm not short of work."

"So, have you come to live here for good?"

"That's the plan. The business is doing well in London with my son and daughter from the first marriage in charge. I will go and come, but most of my time will be here now."

They had been sitting on his veranda one Sunday looking across at her house where Andrew and some of the boys from the area were playing basketball. They were greeting each success with too much noise she had thought.

"'Why aren't you in one of those high-end communities along the elegant corridor?" she had asked him, surveying his strong, bulky, well-defined body and relaxed face.

"There is nothing wrong with this community."

"Of course, I know that. But most of your type prefers the showy places where your big car would be more at home."

He had laughed. Then the conversation had gone silent as they watched the boys play and a couple of girls standing on the pavement assessing the boys.

"People here don't like strangers," she had continued. "Somebody has to bring them in, but no one brought you in. You just appeared."

"Nobody has bothered me. Besides people know you, they love your family, and you are sitting on my veranda drinking limeade with me."

"My protection is within earshot," she had said, looking across the road at her son.

"True. I am watching myself."

Then as if she had just heard all of what he had said, she had asked, "How do you know people love me? What do you know about my family?"

He had continued looking across the narrow road that separated their homes but had not responded. She had watched him tracing the large triangle that his legs formed as his legs were thrown wide apart.

I could do worse if it's just the physical side I'm looking for at the moment.

In fact, his being a stranger had not bothered her. His newness was the reason she had decided to given him a chance. He had not known Rainsford, and Rainsford had not known him. If they had known each other as friends or acquaintances from the community, it would have been like incest. The nagging feeling of disloyalty would have also been another matter.

Without planning, she reached under the bed for a tin containing the letters Rainsford had written to her when he had wanted to date her and while they dated. The thought of how different he was from the other young men still made her heart swell. Who wrote letters on such fine papers and with a fountain pen in the twenty-first century, she thought. And he had not pressed them in her hand; he had sent them through the post. He had written one every week for a year when they were dating, and after she agreed to marry him, one a day for almost a year. She opened the tin but did not pick up any of the letters, just scanned the soft cream colour of the matching envelopes (that each letter had been delivered in) and his unmistakeable curly, right-slanting handwriting. Texting and hurried emails had never been his habit.

More composed than a few minutes earlier, she returned the tin under the bed, locked up the house, and left the yard. She planned to meet Andrew after work to eat. She didn't cook on Fridays, hardly anyone did. Besides, Fridays were her busiest day of the week and after work she usually had no energy to do anything other than sit and be fed, take the taxi home, shower, and go to bed. Everyone wanted to be made fresh for the weekend. Not only was her chair busy but also the chairs of the six women who rented space from her: four did women's hair, one a barber and head-masseuse specialist, and the other a manicurist. The rent from three of them paid her utilities. The rent from the other three plus her own earnings kept her and Andrew and helped her to put aside for his education. It was not easy but it could have been worse, she always told herself.

The taxi pulled up as her cell phone rang Tarrus Riley's "She's Royal." Andrew had put the ringtone on her phone. She glanced at the screen. It was not Andrew but Ancel; she would call him back when she got to the salon. The phone rang again soon after the car pulled away, followed shortly by a text message: "I am at the airport; call me as soon as you get this. A."

She had not seen him for a couple of weeks. He had left saying he would be in Kingston on business for the weekend. He had then called on Sunday to say he was going to another parish (Manchester) and staying in Mandeville with friends for a few days. He wanted to know if anyone had called at his house in his absence.

"How would I know that? I don't spend my time looking at your house."

"You know, I don't mean that. Just wondering if anyone caught your eye."

"No one has," she had said.

Although he had denied it when she quizzed him, she knew that men like him could have more than their share of women. He had a show-of-money persona and a big-and-broad, well-cared-for look that suggested high status. Perhaps he was moving between several women at the moment, she had thought. When he called again at the end of the week to say he would be in the parish of Portland for another few days, she had sniggered.

"Thank God, I don't need to marry again or be with anyone," she had said out loud when he rang off. "If I was in love with him, I would be going mad now."

She had heard women in the salon talk about men playing games like that with them. That had never been her life with Rainsford. It was all new to her, and it left her with an unfamiliar and uncomfortable feeling. She decided she would bring what was left of their relationship to an end when he returned. She was too old for that nonsense.

A nagging disquiet rested on her as she left the taxi and walked up the high street to her salon. She decided not to return his calls or texts when he called again as she mounted the steps to the first floor of her shop. No doubt there was someone in England too, she thought. Annoyed with herself for being unable to get rid of him from her mind, she stopped on the step and responded to his call.

"Where have you been? I have been ringing and texting. Didn't you get them?"

"I was in a taxi. What can be so urgent that it cannot wait?"

"I am off to England."

"What? You have toured all fourteen parishes and now you are going to tour England." Then, remembering he had children, she asked, "Oh! Are the family alright?"

"Yes, yes, yes," he said hastily.

"Gosh. What's wrong? You sound funny."

"Nothing is wrong."

"When will you be back? Is everything off in the house, the water, the gas?" she asked.

"Don't worry about any of that. Look after yourself and Andrew. Miss you already."

She sniggered.

He sucked his teeth audibly. "Do me a favour though. Don't go over to the house or anything like that."

She frowned and raised her voice. "Why the hell would I want to do that when you are not there?"

"Why you so sensitive, Corrine? You know I don't mean anything bad by that. Just keep away from my house. Please. Look after yourself and the boy. Have to turn the phone off now. Bye for now."

She would return the key to his house, which he had insisted she keep, as soon as he got back. She had not wanted to hold it in the first place.

As she mounted the final steep step to the salon, she held the rails mindful of the chipped tiles that were overdue for replacement. She took a deep breath and tried to exorcise Ancel from her mind as she pushed the door open.

There were already clients being tended to and others waiting to be seen. One of her nieces, Lisa, rented a space from her too, and they took turns opening the shop each day. Thankfully, it had been Lisa's turn to open today, with the lack of energy that plagued her since she woke up.

Corrine greeted Lisa, who was already well on her way canerowing the hair of an elderly lady. Her salon, CA & R Hair Specialists (referencing hers, Andrew's, and Rainsford's names), specialised in natural hair care: traditional locks, sista locks, braids, and canerows. Lisa's specialty was canerows and braids, and Corrine's was traditional and sista locks.

Corrine's own hair was the advertisement that had gained her many clients as she moved around Montego Bay and Saint James. Of late, she had done a course in natural hair products and was trying her hand at making hair products with locally sourced cold-pressed coconut oil, herbs, various roots, and essential oils. She hoped to get them approved and licensed to sell in shops and salons within the year.

The radio was on and tuned to their preferred station. The station they preferred specialized in soft reggae, kept them informed of local news, and entertained them throughout the day. There was also a lively discussion about labour pains taking place in the back of the salon, no doubt initiated by the young lady who was having her nails done while gently rocking her baby's carrier with one of her feet.

A man she had not seen at the salon before was sitting by the barber's waiting area. She nodded a greeting. The other workers had not arrived yet but had clients waiting for them. Corrine's first appointment was due any time now.

Corrine's own area was sectioned off from the rest of the salon with a door that could be locked if necessary. The door was often left open, especially when it was particularly hot, so that all the standing and wall fans could circulate air freely. They did not often have the windows facing the main road open because the noise and commotion of the main road made conversation impossible. Sinks for hair washing were towards the back of the large room, and two bathrooms were beyond the sinks. The room was arranged such that she and Lisa had views to the street; the others' chairs were arranged against one of the walls with a waiting area behind each chair.

Corrine did her daily round when she arrived, even though she knew Lisa would have gone over everything. She checked that the bathroom supplies were sufficient for what would be a busy day, that the sinks were clean, and that there was sufficient water in the four-hundred-gallon tank outside on the small balcony in case of water lockout. All were in order. She was headed back to her room when the man she had noticed earlier asked if she was Corrine Gregory, the owner.

"I am, sir. And you are?" she asked.

"They call me Savi. I am here waiting for the barber, but I want to be sure I am in the right place."

She smiled and asked, "Someone recommended the salon?"

"Someone sent me to you," he said.

Corrine smiled with pride.

"'The barber will be here shortly. She tends to work with appointments though. Do you have one?"

He shook his head. She looked at his well-cut hair and assumed he was there for a head massage. Head massage had recently become the most popular job for the barber especially since a local radio announcer enjoyed one and mentioned it and CA & R on the radio. Seeing how popular it had become and predicting that Jean (the barber) would soon leave and set up on her own shop, Corrine took a course to learn the art of head massage. The radio had promoted CA & R, not Jean, so Jean would have to work to get the good reputation that she had fortuitously bestowed upon the salon.

"But don't worry. I'll will fit you in if the barber is not able, especially since you were sent to me," she said, beaming and looking steadily at him.

"OK, I can wait."

"We will take good care of you. Good to meet you, Savi," Corrine said, as she turned to await her first appointment.

Savi was taken aback by Corrine. He had not expected an empress—and such an empress too.

Bushka, who had hired him to kill her, did not know her either and had not described her. Bushka had just told him that she was the owner of the salon and where the shop was on the high street. He knew she was not the actual cause of Bushka's rage.

Bushka had complained to Savi: "Me been hunting her bwooy friend for weeks but me caaan fine him. Every time me hear wey him deh, him move. Me wan you fe mek duppy out of her to teach him to cheat me and dis me." He was furious at the length of time Savi had spent tracking down Corrine's boyfriend to assassinate him.

Savi was known to deliver. He knew his trade. He was more expensive than others like him, so he was only called upon for special circumstances and difficult cases. Unlike some of those in his trade, he would take out anyone for the right price with two exceptions: empresses and children. He usually asked those questions before accepting the job, but this time he had been distracted and lured by the price Bushka was prepared to pay.

He had his game plan: to enter the shop, identify her, have the head massage everyone was raving about, do his job, find somewhere to eat, and then go watch the high school football match. He had been looking forward to the match for weeks.

Now, he was prevaricating. She had taken him off guard with her easy, sweet manner. She was smaller than he had imagined too: only about five feet three inches tall. Her frame was like a child's but everything else about her was all woman—a woman who knew who she was and what she wanted. Her abundant locks trailing over her shoulders to the middle of her back were jet black and well cared for. As she turned to go to her room, he watched as she lifted her hands above her shoulders then grasped, twisted, and pulled her locks into a bun. His eyes followed her hands to her hips, the only part of her body that held any fat. Her hips swayed gently from side to side, a natural movement, it seemed to him, or long practiced. He shook his head, almost indiscernibly.

Savi's grandmother who raised him called him a *fool fool bwooy*, not on account of what he did for a living because she did not know about that. He had been left with her as a little boy when his parents moved to the States in the mid-1980s. They had promised to file papers for him but somehow that never happened. They sent their remittances fortnightly without fail and his grandmother had seen to it that he was well cared for and most importantly that he went to school. To her pride, he passed several subjects. And the grade ten ones and twos he achieved could have gained him a place into community college and then university, but he was never interested in that. "Money is the root of all evil," she warned, as it became clear to her what his true love was.

He quickly made the money he loved; bought large acreages of land packed with old fruit, pimento, and cedar trees, and hired labour to help him grow fruits and vegetables. He sold the fruits and vegetables to the hotels along the North Coast and in Kingston. He sold pimentos to market sellers and occasionally cut down cedars for furniture makers. He built himself what many considered a modest house on the farm that adjoined the community where he was born and raised, where his grandmother still had her house. She lived at the very edge of one side of the district, he at the other with his land stretching well beyond the district.

Savi, wary of praedial larceny, had gone to the shooting range on the west side of the island eventually getting his gun license. It was by accident rather than by design that he found himself into his second trade, as he called it. Someone he grew to know at the range wanted something taken care of and for some reason entrusted him to take care of it. He was stunned by how much he was offered and agreed to take the chance.

As time went on, Savi learnt how to build his own weapons and how to get his hands on weapons that could not be traced back to him. To the delight of his grandmother, Savi had to cut his flowing locks. He would have easily tolerated her chagrin over his locks, but in his second trade, it was easier for him to anonymously slip in and out of areas without them.

In the early days when he was building up his businesses, he was called on and accepted contract jobs in his second trade often, but now he felt he did not need the money, he did not need to take the risk. He had his land, his house, money in various accounts on and outside of the island, and the equipment he needed.

The only vehicles he needed were a tractor and a truck, which he used on his land and to transport goods to the hotels. He bought new vehicles when he wanted and kept the ones he had in good repair. He took taxis and buses for other things. Now, he only did one or two (at the most) jobs a year if it came through a certain known and trusted source.

His grandmother knew how well he had done for himself and how loved and respected he was in their community. She labelled him foolish, not because of anything to do with business, but because of his well-spouted philosophy about women. She refused to call him Saviour or Savi; she called him Aaron as he had been christened. She did not stand on ceremony with him or put him on a pedestal as almost everyone in the community seemed to. She disagreed with almost everything he said and found something to challenge and reprimand him about whenever she saw him.

"You may be a forty-odd-year-old bigshot to your friends, but you are a foolish bwooy to me. How could a woman be royalty just because she wears locks? It's not locks that turn people royal, bwooy," she would say. "What kind of foolishness is that? These days that is just a hair style, not like back in the days of principles."

He had long stopped trying to defend his position with her, trying to tell her that even if locks was just a hair style people who wore them had made that choice among other choices and there was something significant about that.

Savi passed by his grandmother's house most days (unless he was travelling or had been hired to do a job) and listened to her as they ate. She spoke to him as if he were still the little boy she had trained and moulded. He had a helper at home, but to him there was nothing like the taste of her food, especially her soups. On most Saturdays, he did not just pass by but stayed and ate with her. Even though he hardly ate with her during the week, Savi knew she prepared food for him just in case. But Savi's grandmother never wasted the food. If Savi didn't stop by for dinner, she would give it to the district street man who made it his habit to pass by her house every day just in case.

She showed her tenderness towards Savi only when he was leaving to go home, holding him tight to her as she had done when he was a little boy and had come home from school with an upset.

"Bwooy, I love you. Don't get yourself in any trouble. I would not be able to live if anything happen to you."

"Granny, I am safe. Stop your worrying," he would say, hugging her tightly back and finishing with a peck on her forehead. "Lock up the house properly when I leave" were always his parting words, even though he knew full well that only an errant, ignorant stranger passing through would make the mistake of troubling her.

The barber arrived, but as Corrine had suspected, she had a long list of appointments.

As soon as Corrine had pushed open the door and entered the salon, it was as if she had sapped Savi's momentum—her energy had surrounded and enveloped him, imprisoning him in his seat. There was no doubt that Corrine had disturbed his equilibrium. Not many women had that effect on him. He had one "baby-mother." His baby-mother was the only other woman who had had that effect on him. It was usually the woman who made the first move with him. He had always preferred that. He had never been able to call women like his friends did.

Bushka, his employee that day and the only friend he kept, would say, "Ah because you don't want dem to reject you. You ego fragile man. Ah you fragile ego; you no want to hurt."

It was not like Savi to be indecisive about his work. He knew that could be dangerous, get him hurt or even sent to prison. He sat in the salon for over three hours watching the comings and goings—the expertise of the women transforming unkempt hair into eye-catching works of art. Corrine mainly beavered away in her room but passed him now and again when she went to the sink to wash a client's hair.

He tried but could not help following her with his eyes.

"You don't want to go and come back? You look like a man who has a lot to do," she said smiling.

"You right, you know." He sucked his teeth. "I may well take your advice and go and come. I want to watch a high school football match later, and I have to catch a bite."

He caught himself giving too much information away, but he was not terribly concerned because people knew not to talk. Each person in the shop would know he had marked them from the moment he had entered the shop. He knew each face and would be able to recognise them again. He was never in danger from nearby bystanders, no matter what he did, no matter what he said, and no matter how much he gave away—of late, that was the way it had become on the island—killers were at liberty to ply their trade in broad daylight without fear of being caught.

"My son is playing in a match today. I wonder if it's the same one."

"Is it the high school championship finals?"

"Yes," she said, with a beaming smile and a look of pride. "My son is playing in that."

She motioned to the client whose hair she had just washed to take a seat in her room. Her apprentice had just arrived, and she asked her to towel dry the client's hair for her.

"Oh, which school?"

She told him.

"They are the favourite. They are bound to win especially with my big man, Thinker."

She beamed. "Andrew—he is my son."

Savi stood up and laughed loudly. He was not a tall or big man, but he had a booming laugh. The clients and hairdressers all turned to him momentarily.

"That boy is a genius player. Him going to play for Jamaica. Me sure," he emphasized. "I've never seen you at a match."

With a lowered voice, she said, "I know. My husband used to go. Now it brings too much pain, so I make excuses. Not good, I know."

He noticed a shadow come over her face. So she is married and having a man too, he thought.

"Your husband?"

"Late husband," she said, as her voice lowered to a whisper. "He died a few years back."

It was a first for him—being drawn so much into the life of his target.

"The little man will understand."

The tenderness in his voice brought tears again to her cheeks, so she left him hurriedly to go to the bathroom. When she returned, he was still standing up with his hands hanging languidly by his side.

"Hush, hush," he said tenderly, as if soothing a crying baby. "I'm sure he misses you there, but him have plenty of fans and plenty of love when he plays."

He reached out and held her arm.

"I did hear that his father was dead. Sorry to hear that. Try not to take any of it to heart. It will all work out. Your son is a good boy from what I can see. He will make both of you proud."

She made him giddy with her silky gestures: slow, soft, and defined. Each gesture was in a bubble of its own, yet they were drawn together to form a seamless flow. Empress goodness, he thought. In his world of dealings and double dealings, of scams and counter scams, and easy bloodletting he never imagined that someone like her could be fortuitously drawn into it.

Corrine was back in her room. Savi heard her soft laugh and

conversations, but he could not quite make out what she was saying. His phone rang bringing him back to himself. Bushka was on the other end.

"You done yet?"

"Nay," he said, shaking his head as if Bushka could see him emphasise the negative.

"Dem sey de bwooy left on a flight out of the country: New York and then England me hear." Then with emphasis, he stated, "De man leff her and gaan a foreign. Him won't even know she took a shot for him. No bada. Leff de woman alone, you hear."

Savi listened to the expletives on the other end. They both knew that England was well out of his reach. Bushka had to accept that he had lost.

Savi got up and said to no one in particular, "Be back later."

Corrine called out to him. "Come back after the match, please. I will fit you in. I can do the massage too. Please come back."

There was something about him that was drawing her to him. She did not want him to be disappointed, and she wanted to retain him as a client.

As Savi walked down the stairs, the gun strapped to his ankle (camouflaged by his boots and trousers) weighed heavily against his body.

~~ Corrine ~ Andrew ~ Savi ~~

Corrine found herself running to the bathroom again. She did not know why her tears were flowing so easily. She wondered if it had to do with Andrew. Suddenly panicked that something might be wrong with Andrew, she texted him knowing that he would not be able to look at his phone while in class. It crossed her mind to ring the school, but then she thought better of it. What would she say? She had an odd feeling? They would think she was losing her mind. She hoped he would see the text on the way to the park for the match. School ended at two o'clock and the match would start an hour or so later.

Unable to settle, she decided to do what she had done only once before when her husband was in his final days: she called her afternoon clients and rescheduled them. Only one of them insisted upon being seen that day, and she asked her niece to handle the job for her.

She tried Andrew again but did not get him. He would be

surprised to see her at the match. She went into the supermarket and bought ice-cold water, crackers, and cheese to eat at the match. She bought a fresh coconut from a vendor outside the shop, drank the juice, and ate the jelly.

The second half was well under way by the time she got to the park. A lively throng of supporters ringed the park, some sitting on the walls that surrounded it, others standing around the football field. There were a few empty seats probably for sports teachers and local dignitaries. The local media were also there: a photographer from the press and a film crew from the cable station. She found herself a spot next to a group of overly vocal men and looked for Andrew.

She saw Andrew, with a broad smile on his face, take control of the ball. Spectators erupted into shouts of opprobrium or praise, depending upon which end of the pitch they were positioned. Some called out instructions by name.

"Tinker, pass de ball, no."

"Tinker bwooy, see de gaol dey, no? Shoot no bwooy."

Andrew aimed at the gaol from some distance away but missed.

Eventually Corrine discovered that the game was nil all; no one had scored so far. She scanned the crowd trying to find Savi, if only to tell him she would not be returning to the shop but would like to see him there another day. She did not know why or how he had motivated her to leave her shop to watch her son play. It was true that Montego Bay was not particularly big, but it intrigued her that this apparent stranger knew and admired her son. For some reason, she was comforted by the thought that people thought well of her son and recognized his talent.

She was looking intently into the crowd when a roar erupted. As she looked back at the pitch, she saw Andrew leaping around the goal post. He had scored. She cursed herself for having missed it. Forgetting for a moment that she was actually at the grounds and not in front of the TV at home, she thought she could just wait for the instant replay. Shouts and screams echoed around the ground for the goal—for her son.

Moments later as the final whistle sounded, Corrine could not find space to get near the team or Andrew. As she stood there waiting, she rubbed her eye trying to stop the jumping that had abated for a long time but had now returned. Her grandmother used to say, "A jumping left eye means bad news and a jumping right eye, good." Her grandmother had clearly got it wrong, she thought, as she felt a slight tap on her arm. She turned and saw Savi.

"You came, Empress."

She smiled broadly at him. She had always loved that term of endearment and respect that was used to describe women who wore their hair in locks.

"I have to thank you. I had not planned to come, but you encouraged me. My son will be happy that I saw him score and win the match for his team. And my clients will still be there tomorrow."

He looked steadily at her nodding before eventually saying, "Good decision."

"I can't get near him though."

"Everybody loves the way the boy play. He is going to go far."

"I would rather he goes far with his studies. Sports can be so uncertain."

"Wise words. I am sure you encourage him to take his studies seriously."

She nodded. "Of course, and so far he has not given me any cause for concern."

"I didn't think he is the kind of boy who could."

The crowd around Andrew had thinned, and she excused herself and went to her son's side.

"Gosh, Mummy. What a surprise!"

"I saw your goal. That's my boy."

He allowed her to hug him without tensing to push her away.

"I'm glad I'm allowed in front of your fans."

"I am so happy you came, Mum. Remember to take pictures on your phone of the presentation. See you at the shop later. I have to go back to school to get my stuff."

"I'm taking the afternoon off. Come home. I'll get a pizza and we can watch a video. Proud of you, son," she said, as he disappeared into the crowd.

The ground had almost emptied, but Savi was still standing where she had left him.

Savi had watched her with her son and watched her as she walked back towards him. He averted his eyes as if he had not been watching or thinking about Corrine and her son.

"You look happy," he said, as she approached him smiling. "But your left eye is red. You got something in it?"

She shook her head. "It's been jumping all day." She told him what her grandmother used to say.

"I know about grandmothers and their sayings," he said. "I was raised by one, and she still controls my life. In fact, I am going to spend tonight with her at her house."

"You must be a good man if you love and care for your grandmother."

He grunted.

"I suppose this incessant leaping left eye is one of the reasons I thought I had to see my son. I don't know; my day has been odd. Anyway, I suppose I better go. I plan to relax at home until he comes home. I won't be going back to the shop but really look forward to seeing you back there soon. I will give you the head massage myself."

"I look forward to that," he said.

She turned and left.

"Empress."

She stopped and turned to him.

"Look after your son and be safe."

"Thank you," she said. "You too."

He wanted to say, *Don't trust anyone, not even me*, but he thought better of it.

Savi got into a taxi bound for his grandmother's home. He stayed for dinner—Friday was beef soup. He sat on the veranda and ate with her and listened patiently as she found something to reproach him about. At seven o'clock they watched the news. There was nothing on the news about a hairdresser being gunned down in her salon in Montego Bay.

He washed the dishes for his grandmother while listening to her sing as she got ready for bed. He did not go home or meet Bushka to drink in their local rum bar. Instead, Savi sat on his grandmother's veranda basking in the breeze coming off the hills and listening to the crickets and the conflicting noises of barking dogs in the distance. He turned off his phone and sipped the cold beer left for him in the cooler on the floor.

When he had had enough, he went into the room that he had slept in when he was a child—the room that his grandmother still maintained as if he were a child. He slept soundly among his football trophies and school certificates that adorned the room. He had a soothing dream about the swaying hips of Empress and her beautiful locks cascading over her narrow shoulders and down her back.

ABOUT THE AUTHOR

Vernella Fuller was born in Saint Catherine, Jamaica, in 1956. She is the second eldest of six siblings. Her parents immigrated to England in the early 1960s, and she joined them in 1968. During those early years, Vernella was heavily influenced by her mother, Delceta, and her Grandmother Beatrice, both of whom instilled in her a great love for books, reading, and learning.

Vernella attended secondary school in South London and received an undergraduate degree from University of Sussex; a post-graduate teacher certificate from Goldsmiths, University of London; and masters and doctorate degrees from the Institute of Education, University College London.

Vernella taught history and sociology in secondary school and at the college level in London for over seventeen years. She was and remains an educator and advocate for learning and literacy. In the 1990s, she began writing stories and authoring books about the lives of people with British-Jamaican heritage.

In 2007, Vernella permanently returned to Jamaica. She lives in Rose Hall, Saint James.

Also by Vernella Fuller:
Going Back Home
Unlike Normal Women
Returnee

Cover ~ Marie Bann